EMP ANTEDILUVIAN

FEAR

Book 2

S.A. ISON

EMP   ANTEDILUVIAN FEAR

Book Design by Elizabeth Mackey
Book Edited by Ronald Ison Esq. Editing Service
Book Edited by Boyd Editing Service
Book Edited by Wild Woods Editing Service

This is a work of fiction. Names, characters, places and
incidents either are the production of the author's
imagination or used fictitiously, and any resemblance to
locales, events, business establishments, or actual
persons – living or dead- is entirely coincidental.

For My Uncle Ron

Our family historian who keeps our past alive. He reminds us of our old ways. A true Kentuckian.

OTHER BOOKS BY S.A. ISON

BLACK SOUL RISING

**INOCULATION ZERO WELCOME TO THE STONE AGE
BOOK ONE
INOCULATION ZERO WELCOME TO THE AGE OF WAR
BOOK TWO**

**EMP ANTEDILUVIAN PURGE
BOOK 1
EMP ANTEDELUVIAN FEAR
BOOK 2
EMP ANTEDILUVIAN COURAGE
BOOK 3**

**POSEIDON RUSSIAN DOOMSDAY
BOOK ONE
POSEIDON RUBBLE AND ASH
BOOK TWO**

EMP PRIMEVAL

**PUSHED BACK A TIME TRAVELER'S JOURNAL
BOOK ONE**

**PUSHED BACK THE TIME TRAVELER'S DAUGHTERS
BOOK TWO**

EMP DESOLATION

THE LONG WALK HOME

VERMILION STRAIN POST-APOCALYPTIC EXTINCTION

THE HIVE A POST-APOCALYPTIC LIFE

THE MAD DOG EVENT

DISTURBANCE IN THE WAKE

OUT OF TIME AN OLD FASHION WESTERN

NO ONE'S TIME

NO TIME FOR WITCHES

A BONE TO PICK

THE WILDER SIDE OF Z

THE WILDER SIDE OF RAGE

THE WILDER SIDE OF FURY

THE WILDER SIDE OF WAR

THE WILDER SIDE OF HELL

ANCIENT DEATH

CHAPTER ONE

Harry Banks looked around the porch, all eyes were on him and Alan. Harry knew that what he was asking of Alan would be very dangerous, but at this point in time, there was no help for it. They were all in danger, and it was only going to get worse. The teenager, Alan Tate was innocuous enough to move through the town of Beattyville Kentucky, without drawing undue attention upon himself. Because he was young and white, and poor, no one would look twice at him.

His sister, Willene, had taken the orphaned baby, Angela, into the house; he supposed it was to feed the child. No one knew how long Angela Santo had been hidden before her entire family had been hanged. The child's father, mother and older fifteen-year-old brother, Robert, were hung for being Puerto Rican, because they were not white.

Alan was still weeping, though most of the tears had slowed. Harry knew that finding his young friend and his family, so brutally murdered, would scar the young man for the rest of his life. But Alan had found and rescued the baby. Harry knew Willene would take care of her and love her.

His twin sister had always wanted children, but it never seemed to happen for her. In this new world, he knew it more than likely never would, but now there was this baby, Angela. She must have had a guardian angel, to have survived her family's plight. With the advent of what they thought was a solar coronal event, the massive EMP, they speculated it had stopped the world's technology. To add insult to injury, the town's local chapter of the KKK had raised its ugly head and was even now wreaking havoc, with murder and enslavement. Their homegrown terrorists were at play and there was no one to stop them. Their small town was one of thousands across the country. No military had come to their rescue yet and no government as well.

"Listen before you say yes, Alan, listen first. I need you to contact people in town. People you think you can trust with our lives. With your own life. It will be dangerous because you may not know who you can trust," Harry said, looking into the teen's eyes.

"Yeah, I can do that, what do you want me ta do?" Alan asked, wiping his eyes with the handkerchief Harry had given him. Harry could see that Alan was starting to get his strong emotions under control and Harry was glad. Something like this could break anyone, and the kid was so young, to have seen so much violence; he hoped Alan was resilient. Harry knew soldiers that had not been resilient enough to get over the loss of a comrade in arms, age wasn't necessarily a determining factor. They would all have to be resilient, because they could be faced with more losses in the near future.

"We are going to need a lot of people to help us. First, we need to rescue those people in the coal mines; they can't survive down there for very long, especially the women and children," Harry said, still stunned to find out Mayor Audrey and Sheriff Yates had put all non-whites, non-Christians and anyone helping those people, into the coal mines as slave labor.

It didn't matter, women, children, old and young. The mayor and sheriff were trying to take over Beattyville under the flag of the KKK. With the devastation, it seemed to have brought about the very worst in some of the people of their town. Harry didn't know if some folks waited for a disaster to show their true nature, or if the disaster forced them to evolve, or degrade. To want to wreak havoc and destroy all those around them, including themselves, he could not understand. Whatever the case, their lives had been changed by the solar EMP; the world had gone to hell and those bastards were taking advantage of it all.

He'd seen it before in other countries. Any weakness was met by those who would exploit it. He'd fought that while serving in the army. He would fight it now. He didn't like that it was his own countrymen. But evil was evil, it didn't have a color, age, or gender.

He looked around at the faces of the people who'd come to live in his home. Clay Patterson, a policeman with the Beattyville police force, Boggy Hines, a coal miner, and Marilyn Little, a nurse with her seven-year-old son Monroe, they were black and they were in danger. The doctor, Katie Lee was Korean, and their newest addition, Angela Santo, was Puerto Rican. They had all become targets of the new regime. Earl Bayheart, a mechanic and white, he was helping to protect everyone and had come to live with Harry and Willene. Clay and Katie were nearly murdered themselves, but for a timely intervention.

Alan had saved Katie at the hospital, when men came to kill her. They'd already murdered her mother and father, and Alan's valor had continued by saving Angela. *He is a fine young man*, Harry thought.

"Next, we need to take Beattyville back from Audrey and the KKK. We can't have that lowlife murdering at will, and using people as his personal slave labor. We need intel, we need to know how many men and women he has working for him, where they are located, living, gathering in numbers. Who they are and how can we turn the tide. There have to be many more people who are against this lunacy," Harry said.

9

"I can talk ta my grandpa, I expect he'll know some folks and know what to do," Alan said, his mouth and jaw trying to firm up.

"I have a cousin, and he was a Marine, way back when. Maybe you can locate him, I'm sure he has connections as well. His name is Bonaparte Patterson, his friends call him Boney," Clay suggested.

"Thank ya kindly, I'll do that," Alan said, wiping his nose on the handkerchief.

"Also, I'll give you the address of my apartment; I've got a lot of food there. You're more than welcome to it, and if you come this way again, you can bring some of the food and maybe some of my clothes and things if you don't mind," Clay offered.

Harry looked at Clay, then at the thin youth. "That won't be necessary Clay, we have more than enough food here, don't worry. If you want Alan to have it, that's fine, but honestly, we are well set up here. That is a great idea about picking up your personal things, I know you'll be a lot more comfortable with things that fit." Harry grinned at Clay, understanding the need to have your own things around you. Clay was a big man and Harry's clothes didn't quite fit him.

"If you're sure, I really want to help and contribute what I can with the food. Otherwise," he said, looking at Alan. "You're welcome to it. If you find anyone struggling, maybe share with them," Clay said, shrugging his broad shoulders.

"Thank ya, Officer Patterson," Alan said shyly, a soft grin on his homely face, "I'll be sure ta pick some of your things up an' bring them by here, soon as may be."

"Just Clay." Clay smiled at the teen.

"Alan, go home and get things rolling. I will caution you to be very careful though. You won't know who to trust right off, so go slowly. Do not let anyone know who is here, except your grandfather," Harry warned.

"Oh no sir! I ain't tell anyone that. I ain't even told my grandpa where Dr. Katie is," Alan said earnestly.

"Good man," Harry said and grinned.

"Alan, I will follow you in my truck. I need you to take me to the Santo's home. I'll need to gather up all Angela's things, especially diapers and anything else she might need. Clay, I'll go ahead and swing by your place as well and pick up what I can. Alan, I'll also help get the bodies of Angela's family down. I'll bring them back here and we will bury them in back beside my grandfather."

"Thank ya, Harry. I'm much obliged," Alan said, relief suffusing his face.

"Thank you, Harry, I really appreciate you getting my things as well," Clay said.

"Do you think you'll be able to make it back here, Alan?" Katie asked.

"Yes'um, I can try. I can maybe syphon some of that gas from all them abandoned cars. Git me back here," he answered shyly, blushing profusely, the tips of his ears going bright pink.

"I think he should only come at night. I think he'd know if anyone be following him," Boggy suggested, his eyes large and watching. Boggy didn't always say a lot, but Harry knew that when the kid did say something, it was well worth listening to.

"That's a good idea Boggy, from now on Alan, only come at night, and vary the times. Just to make sure no one is following you. Always try to keep in mind, situational awareness," Harry suggested.

"Sure nuff, I'm gonna go now," Alan said and Harry walked with the boy down the hill.

"Give me a minute to get my truck and a tarp to put over the bodies," Harry said. He ran back up to get his keys, and saw Earl coming around from back with a tarp; Earl had read his mind. He grinned, and got into the truck.

"I figured you could use an extra pair o' eyes," Earl said, patting his shotgun.

Harry grinned and got in, "Yeah, I think any more, it'll take a lot of everyone using an extra set of eyes."

When they got to the tree, Harry's stomach turned, and his mouth filled with saliva. He had to swallow a few times to get it under control. He'd seen death before and it was always ugly. He let the anger rise up, and it nearly suffocated him, it also took the nausea away. His eyes narrowed, and his jaw was clinched, the muscles bunching and bulging. His hands ached to punch something, to find the bastards who'd done this horrible thing.

"Lord'a mercy. I don't know how they coulda killed a whole family," Earl said breathlessly, a sob choking his voice.

Harry had to blink back tears, seeing the bodies swing gently in the early evening breeze. He wiped angrily at his eyes. Their grotesque faces turned toward the setting sun, bloated and blackened, their soft hair lifting in the breeze. The loud buzz of heavy bloated flies permeated the air around them. The flies crawling obscenely over the corrupt faces, over the bulging dead eyes, their iridescent purples and blues flashing in the fading light.

A short distance away, in an old bent oak, a murder of crows gathered, cawing their discontent. Their bead black eyes watched the men in interest, their heads cocking back and forth. A few ruffled their feathers then took flight. Harry guessed they'd been about to feast, but coming late. He and Earl were going to take their prize. Harry was glad they'd gotten to the bodies before the crows. The flies were bad enough.

Harry heard Earl retching behind the truck. He swallowed heavily. The air was redolent with decay, heavy and cloying and the incessant buzzing didn't help. He had to look away for a moment; thoughts of writhing maggots in every soft opening filled his mind. He was glad it hadn't gotten that far either. They didn't even look like humans any more.

He walked over to Alan, who'd started weeping again. He placed a hand on the young man's narrow shoulders.

"You're a brave young man Alan, you shouldn't have to face this kind of nightmare at your age. But you have and you've saved two people. I'm sorry again, that your friend and his family were murdered. Let's get them down and we'll make sure they get a proper burial."

Alan nodded and wiped an arm across his face, his large eyes red and swollen. Harry got back into his truck and backed it up, beneath the bodies. He and Alan held each body as Earl cut them down, and they laid them side by side in the bed of the truck. Harry had to clench his eyes shut and hold his breath. He swallowed again and again, feeling the lifeless flaccid flesh beneath his hands. Once they'd been cut down, Harry and Earl secured the tarp over them.

The smell was ungodly and Harry wondered if he'd be able to wash the oily stench from his body and clothes. He and Earl got back in the truck and followed Alan to the Santo's home. As they drove, he and Earl didn't speak. He glanced at Earl, who was looking out the window and he could see the shimmer of tears hanging suspended in the man's eyes.

Harry's own eyes felt dry, because his rage was so high, his body dried the tears that would have been there. He could feel the boiling heat of the savage fury that filled him and washed through him. The inhumanity of it all was staggering. He followed Alan's truck into a small cul-de-sac of cookie cutter homes. He pulled in behind Alan's truck. Harry got out and walked to his truck.

"You'd best get home, you don't want to be seen hanging around here too long. Be careful, keep a low profile and remember situational awareness, be aware of everything and everyone around you."

"I sure will Harry. Thank you," Alan said and reached his hand out to shake Harry's. Harry shook it firmly, using both hands to clasp the younger man's, willing strength into him.

Harry stood in the road for a while as he watched the young man drive away. He knew that it would be dangerous for Alan, there were so many unknowns, but he was hoping that the boy would be overlooked and underestimated. Harry just hoped he hadn't doomed the boy.

"I'll head in, hit the horn if you have any problems," Harry told Earl.

Earl smiled a gummy smile and gave a salute, and Harry thought he still looked a little pale from his earlier episode with retching. He turned and headed into the Santo's home; the door was unlocked. He drew his weapon, and opened the door. When he stepped in, he could immediately detect something foul. He raised his weapon, his eyes narrowing.

The house was dark, and he felt around in his pocket, and found his small LED flashlight. He stood still by the front door, his gaze moving, and illuminated the interior of the house, the light arcing over the room. He tried to pick up any movement or sound. The furniture had been turned over, books had been thrown about the floor and someone had defecated on top of a stack of college books, and several portraits.

Harry shook his head, stepped in, and saw that all the photographs that had been on the wall had also been torn down and thrown about the room. It looked like they'd tried to start a fire, but the pile had only smoldered and had eventually gone out. He moved to the kitchen; all the cabinets were open, dishes had been thrown to the floor and broken. He checked and found no food. He did find some jars of toddler baby food, which had not been broken. He wondered if they'd had a moment of conscience.

He found several empty shopping bags; he placed the jars carefully into the bags. He found paper towels and crumpled up several and used them to cushion the small glass jars. He found some small spoons and dishes and he added those to the bag. He worked his way into the bedrooms. He found the family dog, a small one, it had been stomped to death. That must have been part of the foulness in the house. Someone had defecated on the bed in the master bedroom.

He found some photos of the family on the nightstand, and he placed those in the bag. He went into the bathroom and found toilet paper, shampoos and feminine hygiene items, and placed all of those in the bag. He then went into the boy's room; there wasn't as much damage, though books and papers were strewn around. He found several more photos and put them in the bags. He stood for a moment and looked around. It was a typical teenage boy's room. His heart broke once more for the horror the child went through before his life was ripped so violently from him. The evil deeds men do, it was beyond his comprehension. Sadly, it was nothing new and he'd seen it before in Afghanistan and Iraq.

He headed to Angela's room and looked around; this room was completely untouched. He walked in and saw that she had lots of stuffed animals, dolls, and toys. He went into Robert's room and retrieved the pillowcase from his bed. He went back and began to get diapers, clothes, blankets, toys and other things he thought the child would either need or want later. He wanted to get her things for when she was older, as remembrances of her family. Once he finished, he walked back to the living room. He looked among the family photos that hadn't been desecrated and pulled them from the rubble. He found a photo album and pulled that out as well.

He walked to the door and put his hand on the doorknob. The house was now a shell, there would be no laughter, no love, no family. The men who'd done this had destroyed much more than personal effects; they destroyed a family's legacy, they destroyed a little girl's life, and her family.

☐

Bella May Hogg sat rocking patiently in the cool basement. Her solar lantern brightened the space considerably. She hummed pleasantly to herself as she sipped her soup, it was good, though the meat was a little gamey. The basement was cozy enough, but just a little chilly. The soup warmed her insides delightfully.

It had certainly been a long day but it had ended on an up note. She shook her grizzled head, thinking about the audacity of the nasty young man that had walked into her home earlier that day. The brutal little bastard had cold cocked her, right on her jaw. She moved her jaw experimentally and winced. He'd busted her nose as well, but she was satisfied that it wasn't broken as she flexed and flared her nostrils. Her ability to smell was a little off, but once the swelling went down, she'd be right as rain.

She narrowed her faded green eyes and took another bite of soup. The comfortable rocker-recliner was situated in the basement, which had been built by her late husband, Claud, to her exacting specifications. The useless man had done a good job, but only because she'd kept at him. Many times, in the heat of summer, she'd come down to cook her meals; the kitchen seemed to stay hot. And now, it didn't work at all. The cool basement had now become her *she-shed*.

She lifted her head when she heard a moan. The young man was starting to rouse; a soft smile creased her wrinkled lips. The little peckerwood had toppled her fine oak hutch, breaking many of her prized plates. Her eyes narrowed again in annoyance. It had taken her years to collect those plates. Dirty little worm.

When she'd come to, she'd found most of her precious plates shattered, and the heavy hutch overturned, the greasy man unconscious beneath it. She'd been stymied for a way to remove the jackass from beneath the hutch, and then a spark of brilliance hit her.

She had gone into the garage and found a car jack and she had then placed the jack under the hutch, and lifted the hutch up enough to place supports beneath the heavy furniture. This way, she was able to attach a rope around the noisome man's wrists. He'd been close enough to the basement door to run the rope through the pulley system that Claud had installed many years ago.

Nearly forty-five years ago, she had insisted on having pulleys put into the basement ceiling and on several walls. She had Claud also attach a crank and winch system. She wanted the ability to move things in and out of the basement that were too bulky or too heavy for her. She appreciated the independent ability to do things by herself; the pulley and winch system gave her that freedom.

He'd complained throughout the whole process, but she had badgered and nagged him until she had what she wanted, just how she'd wanted it. Bella May always got what she wanted once she put her mind to it. Her husband was no match for her stubborn streak, which was one of the reasons she'd married him.

Using the rope, pulleys and the crank, she got the unconscious man's body down to the cool basement. Once she had him there, Bella May had stripped him of his grimy clothes and proceeded to thoroughly wash him clean. The man stank like a sewer, and it had been all she could do to keep her gorge down. She'd tossed his filthy clothes out back, into the refuse pile, to be burned later. From upstairs, she got one of her heavy oak chairs, and her jig saw and a drill bit.

Taking the chair below, she proceeded to use the drill to cut a hole in the chair's seat. She then took the jig saw and cut a bigger hole. She was glad she had several batteries that still had their charge. She then used the rope through another pulley and winch system to lever the man onto the chair.

She then placed the chair where she wanted it and chained it to a large vertical steel beam, which supported the upper floor. She had then chained the man around his waist and around his upper chest and under his armpits. There was little wiggle room, she made sure. She had then secured his legs to the heavy chair, above and below the knees. She used heavy duct tape along with smaller chains.

Then she'd bound his arms to the chair's heavy arms and the steel beam behind the chair.

The man was effectively immobilized, she was confident that he was going nowhere fast.

Bella May was nearly finished with her soup when she noticed the man's eyes were blinking open. She sat forward in her recliner and smiled. Her bowl was poised in her lap, her hands cupping it gently.

"Well, hello sunshine," she said, grinning, her cheeks very pink.

The man groaned and blinked rapidly and tried to shift. It took a few moments; she waited patiently, but she saw that he was finally beginning to realize he was secured in place.

"What? What, where, what?" he asked in confusion, his eyes trying to focus themselves. He'd had a cut over his brow, which she had kindly stitched up. She'd been a nurse long ago, and still had some of the tools of her previous trade. She always thought of herself as ready for anything. She didn't always succeed, but she did try.

"You're in my nice basement young man. Do you remember? You broke into my home and you hit me," Bella May prompted, her head nodding.

The man's eyes focused in on her and she could see the brief and fleeting recognition flash through his bloodshot eyes. He turned his eyes around the basement and then back to her. His eyes looked down and then widened with shock.

"Why you got me all trussed up?" the man asked, anger pushing the confusion aside.

"Why son, you broke into my home. My own home. The place where I live, my home," she said angrily, her face becoming blotchy red, her wrinkled lips trembling with indignant rage.

"You assaulted me young man, in my own home. Without any provocation whatsoever, and you broke my precious plates. Why on God's green earth wouldn't I truss you up?" she spat at him, her eyes bulging with resentment and remembered fury. Her wrinkled lips were pulled back into a snarl.

"Your plates?" the man said stupidly, but then his eyes went down to his hands. He screamed, loud and shrill which bounced around the cool basement walls.

Bella May knew it was coming but winced all the same. She really should have put ear plugs in. His agonized screams went a long way in cooling her temper, and brought another smile to her face.

"My hand, my fuckin hand. It's gone. What happen ta my hand? And I'm neked, why am I neked?" the man cried, realizing for the first time that he'd been stripped of his clothes.

"Well young man, I told you, you broke into my home. You really shouldn't have done that. Now you can't leave," she said, with a sweet smile and her old eyes glittered.

"You're gonna keep me prisoner? My arm hurts. You got to let me go," the man cried, his face creased with pain and fear.

"Oh, don't worry young man, your arm is fine. I stitched it up after I cut your hand off. It is clean and you won't get an infection. What's your name by the way?" she asked, her head cocking to the side, her faded brows raised, her green eyes bead bright.

"You cut off my hand?" he screamed, his mouth hanging open and his inflamed eyes bulged out. The color fled from his face and he was a ghostly white.

"Yes, I just said I did, didn't I and I also cleaned the wound and sewed it up. What is your name young man?" Bella May asked again, thinking this man was clearly a simpleton. She'd seen his teeth and suspected he used drugs, which clearly ate his brain.

"Name's Hobo an why'd you cut off my hand?" Hobo asked, tears now coursing down his cheeks. She could now see the fear in his eyes clearly as they rolled around like a cow waiting for slaughter.

"Hobo, what a name you have." She laughed hard and started coughing, and she smacked her knee, rocking back and forth, tears sliding down her cheeks.

"It's short for Hobart. Why, why would you cut off my hand?" Hobo cried.

"Well Hobo, it needed to be done. See, I need a lot of protein, I always have. And when the electricity stopped, well, all the meat in my freezer went bad," she said, taking another bite of her soup.

"What? What do ya mean?" Hobo asked, looking at her and then his stump.

Bella May smiled once more, *this poor boy is just stupid*, she thought. She shook her head and laughed to herself.

"I'm getting on in years, I'm not as young and strong as I once was. I did all my own hunting years ago, but now, I can only catch the occasional prey. It's become harder now, and less frequent, but I'd set aside meat in my freezer, but with no power, it has become nearly impossible. You came where you shouldn't have come," she explained.

"Lady, what the hell is you talking about?" Hobo screamed, and she winced again.

Sighing heavily, she got up from her lounger and went over to a long table. The table held a single burner portable propane stove. On the stove was a large pot, steam curling out into the cool air. She took the long ladle that rested within the pot and poured more of the chunky soup in her bowl.

She inhaled beatifically and smiled, then walked over to the chained man. Looking down at him she showed him her bowl of soup. He looked down in the bowl and his stomach growled loudly.

She laughed, "hungry, are we? I make a mean soup, put lots of veggies in it and spice it up a bit. The secret is adding smoked paprika. Sadly, the meat is a little gamey, but we can fix that."

Hobo looked into her eyes, and she waited, but he still wasn't getting it. She shook her head; this man really was a dullard.

"Hobo dear, I don't mean to be cruel, but you weren't the brightest bulb in the pack in school, were you? Dear, you're my protein, and this wonderful soup is courtesy of your hand," she said, her eyes bright now, with an inner glow.

Hobo screamed and screamed, horror written all over his face, and she winced, but was smiling broadly now, the dawning realization washed over the man's face like an awful incoming tide.

"Who are you?" he screamed, tears cascading down his contorted face.

"You don't recognize me Hobo? Why I'm Karma." She laughed loudly, filling the basement.

CHAPTER TWO

Harry arrived back at the house with several bags of Angela's things. He'd also packed Clay's suitcase, he'd found in a closet, with clothing and shoes, toiletry items. The apartment had been ransacked, and much of the food stores were gone. Thankfully, most of Clay's personal items had been left untouched. He'd gone through closets and drawers, looking for anything he thought Clay would want.

He also got Clay's photo albums and a few personal effects that would mean a lot to the man. He found a few books and brought those as well. He would make another run and pick up more. He was afraid to take Clay, since he would be a target for murder. Harry wouldn't take that chance for material things.

He'd gotten all of the baby's things and he was glad. Harry wanted the child to know that she'd been loved before her parents were murdered. She'd grow out of the clothes, but she'd always have the photos and they'd make sure to keep some of the toys for her.

Willene was in the kitchen; she said that Clay and Boggy had taken shovels and gone out back, by their grandfather's grave.

"They are diggin a single large hole. It has been slow going, since Clay is still recovering. Boggy, Marilyn and Katie are working with him. How did it go with everything?" she asked, holding the baby, who was asleep in her arms. Her body swayed from side to side and she kissed the top of the child's head. Monroe was at the table eating dinner.

"Well as can be expected. I just stopped to drop off Angela's things and also Clay's. I'm going to take the truck around back, Earl's out there waiting for me. The bodies will have to be cleaned, Willy. It was really bad," he said, looking over at the small boy, who was eating some kind of macaroni dish. There were several candles and lanterns lit in the kitchen, the soft flickering light moved around the room.

"I can't even imagine, Harry, I'm sorry for all of us, to have to live in such a hateful world now. Especially for the children. They shouldn't be burdened with that," she said, shaking her head.

Harry walked up and laid a hand on the sleeping child's small head. Her hair was soft, and her cheeks gently rounded. He smiled at his sister. He walked over to Monroe and made his hand into a claw and lowered it to the boy's head making machine noises, causing Monroe to giggle, and pull his shoulders up to his ears.

Harry leaned over and kissed the top of the boy's head and turned to his sister. "Since the bodies will need washing, I'll have Marilyn or Katie come get the water and some rags. I'd like to clean them up before we put them in the ground," he said solemnly. At her silent nod, he left the kitchen and went out of the house.

Harry drove the truck up into the back of the house, and into the back yard. He drove up the small hill to the gravesite. He was glad the ground wasn't slick. He could see several lanterns lit around the grave site. Earl got out and walked over to look down in the hole. He looked back at Harry and jerked his head.

"Spect I'd best help, that hole ain't deep enough yet."

Harry grabbed Boggy's shovel and hopped down into the hole. "Marilyn, can you and Katie clean the bodies while we get this done, please? I'd hate to bury them like they are now. Willene is getting hot water and rags ready if you want to get them," he said softly.

Marilyn held her hand to her nose and mouth and nodded, her eyes full of tears. She walked away toward the house. Katie came over and looked into the back of the truck.

"My god, those poor people. I just can't get used to the hate. Hate that would hang a child," she said, her voice quavering, her dark eyes filling with tears.

Clay walked over; he placed his large hand over her smaller one. Harry turned away and began shoveling dirt out of the hole. They needed it deep enough, disease could easily raise its ugly head. They were in a world that could no longer fight the old sicknesses, typhoid, tetanus, small pox, mumps, measles and every other illness. They also didn't need scavengers digging up the bodies, nor the dogs. There were a few rocks scattered around, and he figured they could use those to put over the grave, to help keep it covered and safe.

☐

Marilyn returned some time later with a bucket of hot steaming water, some rags, rubber gloves, and masks. Katie got up in the back of the truck; Clay helped her up and then Marilyn. Willene was walking up toward the gravesite; she had an armload of old sheets.

"The kids are in bed and asleep. I figured I'd bring some old sheets to wrap the bodies in," she said, laying them on the tailgate. She hopped into the back of the bed of the old truck. She picked up the gloves and mask. They stripped the bodies, their hands slow and careful. Marilyn had a difficult time holding her tears back. She could see the child in the teen, through the distortion of his corrupt face.

She thought, *this could be us, this could be Monroe.* She felt a shiver go through her. Had it not been for Harry and Willene, they might be in that same state. Had it not been for Harry's foresight, they might well be dead.

"Are you okay Marilyn?" Willene asked softly.

"Yeah, I guess. It's just that, these poor people. I can't help think that this could have happened to my son and me," she said, her voice trembling.

"But it didn't. You and Monroe are safe. None of us will let anything happen to you. You know this," Willene said and laid her gloved hand over Marilyn's arm.

Marilyn smiled beneath her mask, and nodded, then turned back to cleaning the bodies. They stripped off the clothing that had been bloodied and soiled. The clothes would be put into the bottom of the grave.

It was difficult to cut the rope from the swollen hands and away from around the distended necks. Marilyn gritted her teeth, going slow with the scissors. The skin was splitting, seeping and oozing with foul fluids. It took time, but they finished cleaning the bodies then wrapped the corpses in the sheets. Katie and Willene rolled the bodies and she pulled and tucked the sheets.

Harry and Boggy lifted the bodies and lowered them to Clay and Earl, who were standing in the hole. There was a short ladder leaning inside the hole, and they handed it up to make room for the bodies.

Once the bodies had been placed in the grave, Earl and Clay got out of the grave with Boggy's and Harry's help. Harry began to shovel dirt into the grave. Then Clay picked up a shovel and joined him. It took a while to fill in, Earl and Boggy taking turns to help refill the hole.

Once it was done, all stood around the dark grave; it was pitch-black outside but for three lanterns that glowed softly around the grave. The soft chirping of the crickets filled the soft night air. The group was silent but for the muffled weeping of the women. Earl sniffed loudly and blew his nose into an old checkered handkerchief. Marilyn knew Earl had a tender heart; he'd been wonderful with Monroe. It broke her heart to stand there, nearly a whole family annihilated by hate.

"Lord, watch over them poor an' wretched souls, they didn't deserve this. There are evil men an' doin evil things. We got their young 'un, who now is gonna be ours. And we all watch over and protect our young 'uns with our very lives. Amen," Boggy said, his voice cracking with a sob.

Marilyn wrapped her arm around his narrow shoulders. She hugged the young man to her, trying to comfort him. There could be no real comfort for any of them, and not for this family.

Willene sat in the porch swing; the late-night air was cool and crisp. She had wrapped Angela in a soft blanket. Harry sat beside her holding the sleeping baby. There was a full moon and it cast pale light onto Harry's face. His expression was soft as he gazed down at the sleeping child. The day before seemed like a nightmare, putting Angela's parents and brother into the ground. She could still smell the decay on her hands, though she knew it was only her imagination. They'd worn rubber gloves. Perhaps it was stuck in her nostrils. She took a deep breath and blew it out slowly. She'd washed her hands several times after and throughout today, but still she smelled it.

Marilyn sat in a rocking chair, as did Earl, who was smoking his pipe. Katie and Clay sat in the glider, and Boggy was sitting on the floor of the porch, his long legs dangling off the edge. He had the NVGs and periodically looked through them. Monroe was asleep upstairs. The night was quiet but for the sounds of the tree frogs and crickets, the soft susurrus of the wind as it wound through the leaves of the trees.

Earlier that day, Willene fed Angela and had
given her to Marilyn while she went into the attic
to find the boxes filled with old baby clothes and
other baby items. The attic was filled with well-
marked boxes, both by her mother and
grandfather. The boxes were organized by year,
she'd laughed, they didn't throw out much.

With her LED headlamp, she pushed and
shoved the boxes around in the massive attic. It
took nearly an hour, and she'd been covered in
dust and cobwebs, but she found what she'd been
looking for. She sat back on her heels and sighed
happily. A soft smile lit her face and she wiped at
the sweat on her forehead, smearing dust across it,
making muddy streaks.

Because they'd not had much money back
then, her mother had used cloth diapers on her and
her brother. Her mother laughed about the stinky
things, but said she thought the twins were
healthier for it. She changed them more often than
she would have if she'd used disposable diapers.

She smiled when she found old pictures of her
and her brother. She found old toys that she
vaguely remembered. She also found old games,
like Monopoly and Trivial Pursuit. She set those
aside to take below, it would be nice to have a
rousing game night every now and then.
Entertainment was in short supply and it would be
nice to laugh and do something that wasn't linked

to survival. She even found an old Yahtzee game and laughed. She and her brother would argue over the game. They would laugh and accuse each other of cheating. Fixing the dice.

Willene yelled down from the attic, calling Harry to come join her. He came and laughed at all the things she'd pulled out. He picked up the Yahtzee game and waggled his eyebrows. She sniggered and had Harry haul several boxes down and put them in her room. She'd got the diapers and changed the toddler, who's bottom was still red from the long time she'd sat in her own mess.

There were quite a few disposable diapers, but Willene planned to use those solely at night. Yesterday, she and Marilyn had cleaned Angela up, giving her a warm bubble bath in the kitchen sink. The child was enchanted with the bubbles. Katie checked her out, to ensure that she was healthy. They put salve on the child and diapered her with a clean kitchen dish towel.

Willene felt calm; she'd thought she'd be overwhelmed with having a toddler in the house, but it wasn't so. She'd wanted a child for so long and fell easily into the role of motherhood. She seemed to know what the baby needed, an innate understanding. She was already falling in love with the baby.

As far as she could tell, Angela suffered no trauma from her experience, though that might show up later on in her young life. She was almost sure the child was hidden before the violent act. Once more, only time would tell. She hoped for Angela's sake, she'd suffer no psychological long-term effects.

Once Angela had been cleaned up, her small butt salved and powdered, she was fed once more. Since she was old enough, they fed her regular food, some oatmeal and fried apples, which Angela loved. Willene had also made powdered milk and fed the thirsty baby. It might take a few days to get her hydrated properly.

She'd eaten well today, and seemed no worse for her terrible circumstances. Willene let her walk and explore the house, holding her tiny hand as they walked down the stairs. Angela didn't seem to understand the absence of her family, and Willene knew that child would never remember them. That broke her heart most of all. To be so completely forgotten.

Tonight, they had made mashed potatoes, fried rabbit, green beans, dandelion greens and fried apples. Angela had eaten gleefully, much of the food ending up in her soft dark curls. Willene smiled to herself at the memory.

Replete, the child had passed out and hadn't moved since. She'd been passed from one person to another, each wanting to hold her. Her soft rounded cheek pressed into Harry's chest; he had her now.

"You wouldn't think they'd be so heavy when they sleep," Harry said in wonder, his face tilted down.

"Well, she's a healthy little thing, thank the lord Jesus on the ever lovin cross. Or she'd have been in worse shape. I think she'd been there for only a day, it's a miracle something didn't come along and hurt her," Willene said, wiping a stray hair from her eyes.

"That's true and it was also good that it hadn't rained, or she'd might have died from exposure," Marilyn added softly into the dark, the soft creaking from her rocking nearly hiding her words.

"She's safe with us now, that's certain for sure. I think she's got many mommas now," Boggy said, his head twisted around.

"Yep, that's certain for sure," Earl echoed.

Willene hid a grin; she'd known Earl for years, but had never known he had a soft heart. The more she got to know the man, the more she liked and respected him. She knew he'd come from a hard life and an unkind family; she knew his parents had been alcoholics and abusive.

He'd stepped up to the plate though, and she was glad he was a member of their house now. Monroe seemed very attached and stuck close to him. Monroe was a sweet child; Marilyn had done a wonderful job with raising him. Monroe chattered like a magpie but Earl never seemed to mind. The child gravitated to the man and Earl showed Monroe how to work around the farmhouse, explaining things very patiently and allowing the young boy to help whenever he could.

Willene observed them together and laughed. When Earl walked, he limped, but near the end of the day, he limped heavily, she guessed the pain in his leg was more prevalent. The boy would hold his hand, as though helping Earl along, each chatting to the other. Marilyn would stand with her and they'd watch them out in the garden. Earl pointing at this or that. They couldn't hear them, but you could see Monroe was paying attention.

"Who knew Earl could be such a wonderful role model?" Willene said, chuckling.

"I'll swear, Monroe loves that man. I'm glad he has someone who will teach him things. Harry is good to him too, and Clay and Boggy, it is like he has many fathers," she said and smiled. Willene had put her arm around Marilyn and hugged her.

"I imagine, we've become one big family," she said.

Willene batted at a lightning bug that had flown near her face. They were out twinkling in the yard, and made it look magical. She could smell rain in the air, but didn't think it would come any time soon.

"I'm glad you found all those baby clothes and diapers. I was thinking about giving them all a good washing tomorrow," Katie said from the glider.

Willene laughed, she and Katie were usually on the same wavelength. "I was thinking the same thing."

"I need my clothes warshed too. Maybe I can warsh mine?" Earl asked shyly.

The women on the porch burst out laughing, and Earl ducked his head. Willene rocked forward, putting her hands on her knees.

"It isn't you Earl, just a joke about men washing their own clothes," Willene assured the man, and the women laughed harder. It felt so good to laugh, it released the hurtful feelings, Willene felt they all needed a good laugh.

Earl grinned nervously, but had the distinct hunted look that many men sported when a group of women cackled. His look provoked another peal of laughter from the women. Willene noticed the other men were quiet, staying out of the line of fire.

Willene wiped her eyes, and stood; she reached for Angela and she took note that Harry was reluctant to give her up. She grinned at her twin, "I'll pass her back to you when you wake me for my shift," she assured him.

"You sure you want to stand watch?" Harry asked.

"I sure do, and we can all take turns watching her. I'm glad we found that playpen, I wish mom had kept the crib," she said.

"I'll look in the barn tomorrow, it might be stored up in the hayloft. I know Peapot put a lot of things up there over the years. I can look," Harry suggested.

"Sounds good, night y'all," Willene said, taking the baby. She heard the goodnights as she went into the house.

☐

Mary Deets laid on her pallet weeping. Someone had stolen her food. She'd been nauseated earlier and so had held on to her meager breakfast. She'd fallen asleep, but when she'd awaken, her food was gone. Who would steal from a pregnant woman?

She felt someone near and asked, "who is there?"

"It's me, Julie. Are you okay Mary? Is the baby okay?" Julie Elliot asked, worry in her disembodied voice.

"Someone stole my food, I was queasy earlier, and when I woke up, it was gone. I don't know why I'm crying. It is just that being in this dank black hole, it was the only thing to keep my spirits up. Now I have to worry about eating enough for me and the baby," Mary explained, her voice a little wobbly.

"What in the wild world? Who would do that? Hold on, let me see what I can do," Julie said and moved away.

Mary Lou Jaspers came up to Mary and squatted near the woman. Mary Lou reached out a hand and gave Mary a small withered apple.

"Here honey, eat this until we can figure something out. I can't believe someone would steal from you. What is wrong with folks?" the invisible voice pondered angrily.

Mary sat in her bundle of bedding in the dark, there was a light flickering about twenty feet away, and it did little to dispel the crushing darkness in the coal mine.

"Thank you, Mary Lou, that's very kind of you." She began to nibble on the apple. Though it was shriveled, it still had sweetness to it. It helped ease the hunger in her stomach.

She heard feet shuffling and she waited for them to draw closer, only seeing dark shapes.

"Mary, it's David, when did this happen, do you know?" David Colman, a giant of a man, asked. He'd been watching over Mary; her own husband Howard had been murdered by his boss, Sheriff Danny Yates. Because she and her husband were black, her husband had been killed and she'd been put down in the godforsaken hole.

"I'm not sure David, when you gave me the food, I had tried to eat it, but I just felt too queasy to eat more than a couple bites. I put the food, wrapped in the paper towel by my head. I just laid down for a while and then must have fallen asleep. I just woke a bit ago, so I don't know how long I'd been asleep," she said, feeling better with the bit of apple in her and now that David was there. She'd come to depend on and trust him; he was a kind man and she was grateful he watched over her.

"That's been about five hours Mary, it is near lunch. They should be sending food down shortly, so don't you fret none. I'll look into who is stealing food, though I do have my suspicions," he said darkly.

Mary reached a blind hand out and touched David's massive arm, and her hand slid down to clutch his large hand.

"Thank you, David. I just want this baby to be okay. There isn't much food, and I know people are hungry. I'd have shared with them if they'd just asked," she said softly.

David's other hand patted her own, "Don't you worry Mary, I'll make sure you get your food and that you're kept safe. I won't let anyone harm you or your baby," he promised, his deep voice soft and soothing.

She brought his large hand to her cheek and pressed it there for a moment. She let it go and heard the big man shuffle away.

"If anyone can find out who is stealing, it's David. He'd been that security guard at the bank, I guess he can find a thief easily enough," Mary Lou said, and Mary heard the satisfaction and smile in Mary Lou's voice. She smiled as well. She'd remembered seeing David at the bank, and he always had an easy smile for everyone. She had noticed that the disreputable looking people seemed uneasy around him. She smiled at that thought.

She heard the familiar squeal of ropes, cables and gears which heralded the lowering of the food. Their request for more food was heeded, though it wasn't much more. A few minutes later, Julia returned with food, wrapped up. It was bread, cheese and a fruit cup. Milk had been brought as well.

Mary thanked her and lifted her mask and began to eat slowly. She wanted to make it last. She felt the nausea begin to niggle her stomach, but fought it; her baby needed food. The earlier apple helped as well and Mary thought on the kindness of Mary Lou; she'd worked for the mayor. Everyone had heard how the mayor had fired her, or rather kicked her out of his office. Their world changed so fast.

She took another bite. Now more than ever, she was afraid if she didn't eat it now, she wouldn't have it later. She hoped that none of the children were doing without.

☐

Robby Rob sat in a small grotto that had been chiseled out of the rock, sometime in the long past. He pulled several bundles of food out of his shirt. He'd spent the morning slinking around the sleeping people, taking what he could find among them. If they were too stupid to leave uneaten food about, then it was all the better for him.

He ate a chunk of dried-up bread hungrily. He'd been partying and drugging for so long, that he'd neglected to eat real food. When those white bastards caught him and thrown him down in this stinking coal mine, it had taken a day or two for his body to stop craving drugs and alcohol and start craving food. Now it was painful not having something in his gut. Almost as bad as not having anything to drink. Damn them.

They expected him to work, to do hard damned labor. While all those women and kids sat on their asses and did nothing but eat. Well, if he had to work, he'd eat, and he'd eat their food too. There was a big man, they called him Hercules, but he thought his name was David. He'd seen the man at the bank. Him and that cop, Stroh, thought they could make him work.

He'd gone with them, but he'd not worked. He chuckled softly at the thought. He'd gone through the motions, pretended to do the work, but he'd found places to hide. He was hidden now, eating his stolen food. He then pulled out two withered apples, at least he thought they were apples. It was pitch black, and he couldn't see anything. He'd turned off his headlamp to stay hidden, he dared not turn it on and give himself away.

He heard footsteps and paused, waiting for them to pass. Once they did, he continued to eat. He finished the apples, core and all. He then pulled out a carton of milk. He made a face, it was warm, from the heat of his body. He drank it anyway, he needed the calories. He belched softly and pulled out another bundle. This one had a granola bar in it with a pack of crackers. He finished those off quickly.

He was still hungry but he'd have to wait, food would come in a bit, and he'd make his way back. He'd also make sure he'd get more from the useless kids and women. They were easy targets; they slept all the time. What a waste of food, he deserved it more.

He sat back in his small grotto and got as comfortable as he could. An uncontrollable shiver wracked his body; he would have killed to get a fix. He didn't care if it was booze or drugs, just something to make the pain in his body go away. The food had helped, but his body craved something more. Maybe he could corner one of the women, it didn't matter who it was, just someone to get off on. He'd have to hunt around, find a woman who was farther away from the group and the light. He'd not want to get caught or have some husband hunt him down.

He had to think of a way to get out of this hole. He didn't deserve to be here. Those damned KKK, bunch of no-good pecker-head white boys. And what was this shit about an EMP? He didn't understand what everyone was talking about. They said that maybe North Korea had bombed them, or Russia or Iraq. Somebody send a bomb? He didn't hear no explosion. Maybe those KKK assholes were just telling everybody a bunch of shit, making them believe it. He wasn't that gullible, but he'd get out of here, one way or another.

No, he had to get out of here, no matter what it took. He wondered where Hobo was; he thought the man had the better part of this deal. He was probably out drinking somewhere or getting a good buzz. Damn it, he wished he were with Hobo right about now.

CHAPTER THREE

Willene sat on the porch; the night air had a chill in it. The windows of the farmhouse were open, letting in the breeze through the house. She held up the NVGs and looked around. Nothing stirred. Though hell had come, the night suggested a tranquility and she reveled in it. She would take it where she could get it. They'd been lucky so far. She knew that luck would be short lived. Soon, people would be coming their way. Soon, there would be more killing.

She got up and headed to the rear of the house; she strolled quietly. She heard a whippoorwill calling softly, deep within the dark woods. The ground was damp beneath her feet. She saw a shape in the dark and her heart slammed into her chest. Her hands trembled as she brought up the NGVs and she let out a shuddering breath, it was Clay.

He was walking very slowly, and then she saw his dog following him. She strode toward him, her heart slowing. The adrenaline beginning to recede, making her slightly light headed.

"You should be in bed Clay. I don't think wandering around in the dark is healthy. If you trip or fall, you could rip your wounds open," she said softly.

47

"I couldn't sleep. I keep thinking about that poor family we buried," he said. He joined her as they ambled the perimeter of the large yard. Their steps slow and careful.

"What do you think will happen to us Willene? I mean in the future," he asked, his voice deep and slow.

"Live I guess, live and go on. Though I'm hoping without the threat of the KKK. Life will go on, at a slower pace. It will be driven by the seasons, how we grow our food and hunt. Like the old days, before technology." She shrugged.

"You don't think we'll ever get the power back on?"

She heard the unease in his voice, "Clay, in the course of the next few weeks and months, people will be running out of food, if they haven't already. The people who might know how to fix the problems of power and electricity may already be dead. Especially, if they live in the cities," she said, and shrugged. It was difficult to think about so many people who would starve to death and who were already dead; the numbers would be staggering, and even more so in the days to come. She knew the biggest cities would feel the massive die off first, they had the highest populations.

"It just seems so unreal, so hard to believe that all over the country and all over the world, people who have the knowledge to fix things may be dead. Or will die, because they can't get food, or don't have access to transportation to get food," Clay said.

"With their deaths, the knowledge dies. They may one day repair it, and rebuild, but we are so remote here. We would be one of the last to see it come our way. I have no idea the extent of the damage. I don't know a lot about electrical grids or the turbines and equipment that produce it. We think the solar eruption has fried every electronic circuit," Willene said.

"Yeah, you're right Willene. I was just hoping that maybe someone would at least be trying to get things back up. And yeah, I know, they probably are trying, or at least I hope they are. The military may be able to get things done, but they may have to fight with the people in the cities. I have a sick feeling, people are going crazy there. No food coming in and it has turned into every man for themselves. Even here, the killing started fast."

"Combine that with the disease that will come with massive die offs, especially in large urban areas and cities. Even now, those big cities could be at war, killing each other for a can of dogfood. And no burials, not for that many people. Cholera may well be brewing," Willene said, sadness and muted horror in her voice.

They stopped and she put the NVGs up to her face and scanned around. She saw the dog once more go off into the woods, she knew Charley was asleep with Monroe. She wondered if Brian was hunting small game.

"I'd say you were one of the rare people that had food put away. Most people don't, I'm pretty sure, most people don't know how to hunt, or grow vegetables. They don't know how to survive. There are quite a lot of people who lived on ready-made food, boxed food and takeout. We are now getting into the time where whatever they had in their pantries is running out. So, if they can't find anything, they'll die or kill others to get what they need," she said, trying to keep the emotion out of her voice.

"All things considered, I'm damn glad to be here. Tonight, I want to start standing watch. I have been walking around for a bit, and though I still hurt, I feel better and stronger."

"Sounds good to me, I'll let Harry know and we can work you into the rotation. It will be nice, that means we can each get a whole night off at some point." Willene grinned upon hearing his soft chuckle.

"Go to bed Clay, let your mind and your body heal, it will be morning soon enough," Willene advised when they came back around to the front of the farmhouse.

"Sure nuff, night Willene, see you in the morning," Clay said and disappeared into the darkness of the house.

Willene went to sit in the swing; she moved slowly back and forth, using the NVGs to look around. It was quiet, but she knew that would be short lived soon. People would be moving this way, looking for food and that was when the real fun would begin.

☐

Alan sat at the kitchen table with his grandfather, Wilber Tate. Both ate quietly; Alan made oatmeal and fried up a couple of eggs. The bacon was gone, but there was still bread, though it was a little stale. Butter sat in a round crock and homemade jam helped the bread considerably. They sat in companionable silence.

Alan came home the other evening, weeping. Wilber had been alarmed, and his grandson told him about the Santo family and about the baby he'd found. Wilber held his grandson, unable to speak himself, between the rage he felt and the grief that choked him.

"How ya feelin grandson?" Wilber asked the boy conversationally.

"I'm okay Pop Pop, I was wanting to ask ya about what we could do, you know, ta help these folks. There's gotta be a way," Alan said, his face and voice solemn.

"Well, I've been ponderin on that very thing. I've got my friends, they're old, but they're capable," Wilber said.

"I was supposed ta ask if you'd know Boney Patterson, heard tell he was a sniper in that Vietnam war," Alan said, taking another bite of oatmeal.

Wilber grinned, his friend Boney had a reputation, "Yes, he sure do, and I'm gonna go to see him today. You can come along with me."

"Thanks Pop Pop, I need ta do something, I just can't sit round and do nothin," Alan said, a soft smile on his sad face.

Wilber reached over with his spotted arthritic hand and patted his grandson gently. "Don't worry grandson, we'll kick them sonbitches asses. They won't know what hit em." He grinned a gummy grin and laughed, his teeth still in a glass.

☐

Gerhard Friedhof stood in the mayor's outer office, shifting restlessly from one foot to the other. The sheriff was in the office with Mayor Audrey, and he could hear their murmuring. Gerhard had come to the sheriff asking for help on his farm. Since the power had gone out, none of his big equipment worked and he had crops in the fields that needed tending, some ready for harvest. If he didn't get help, he'd lose much of the food. Not only that, people had been sneaking onto his lands and stealing the food. He had a large family to feed and he also had field hands and their families. He would be willing to share, but he had to have something to harvest in order to share.

The door opened and Sheriff Yates waved him in. Gerhard was a thin wiry man, and his clothes were usually much too large on him. His head poked out of the collar of his shirt like a turtle's head coming out to investigate. This was made more apparent when his head entered into the office long before his body followed.

"Come on in Gerhard, have a seat," Audrey said, waving the thin man over to an open chair.

Yates sat down beside Gerhard and smiled at the man encouragingly.

"Well, Mayor..." he began, but Audrey stopped him, lifting a pudgy hand.

"I've decided to change my title to President, I think it has a more impressive connotation. I'm going to put out a declaration in a couple days. Sheriff Yates will be our new Vice President." He grinned a wide toothy grin, his crooked teeth yellow.

Gerhard blinked, unsure what to say, so he nodded. "Well, President Audrey, I got a lot of produce that's a comin' near to harvesting. I got people sneaking on my land, and they're stealin' me blind. I can't harvest without my machinery, and I need help," he said, his breath going out in a gush.

"I hear you clear enough, I think we can help you Gerhard. We got some folks in the coal mine that might appreciate being outside that mine, and working your farm," President Audrey said, a wolfish beatific smile slid across his face.

"You can't mean like old time slave labor, President?" Gerhard asked horrified.

"Why sure, Gerhard, we got to put these people to work if they wanna live. Otherwise, I'd just execute them all. Is that what you want Gerhard, want me to just go on and kill these folks? Or do you want help, and they get fed good? I'll leave it to you to decide their fate." Audrey grinned an oily smile.

"I ain't want nobody to die, Lord help me. I just need help with my crops," Gerhard said, his voice rose and sweat popped out on his forehead and his head retreated back down into his collar, his eyes large and looking around the office for an escape.

"Well then, the matter is settled, they live and they're gonna help you with your farm. Now, because you'll be getting these extra hands, you be turning over the majority of the crops to the town. I'll have my men come along and guard the prisoners and make sure nobody is gonna steal from your farm," President Audrey declared brightly, standing up and walking toward the door.

Gerhard scrambled up from his chair, nearly tripping in the process, he ducked his head and bowed at the same time, not sure what protocol was called for. He was so addled, he ran into the door jam, and bounced off and staggered.

"Careful there Gerhard, wouldn't want to knock yourself out." Vice President Yates laughed, and helped lead the man out of the building, his hand under Gerhard's elbow.

Gerhard walked down the steps of the building on rubbery legs and stood looking around on the sidewalk. He shook violently, fear and confusion battling for control of his body and mind. It was frightening, the way they'd looked at him. It was like they were almost insane. They were smiling, but their smiles were those of an alligator or a snake. He'd felt the hair raise all over his body in primordial fear. His primitive brain knew danger when it was near, and they were dangerous, no matter how much they smiled at him.

He'd only wanted help with his farm; he had only wanted to save the food that would rot out there, and waste away. He'd not wanted slaves for heaven sakes. Why had they put the lives of the people in his hands? Why had they made him choose the fate of those poor people? Slaves for

55

Christ's sake. What in the world had Beattyville come to? And President? Vice President?

Gerhard had been sure things would go back to normal soon. That the government would help them get their power back. It hadn't happened, and he and his people had struggled to keep the crops going, but without the equipment, it was just too much.

Gerhard knew he'd not even make a profit, but he certainly didn't want the food in the fields to just rot and fertilize the field. Many people were hungry now, some showing up at his farm. He'd done the best he could and given them some of the ripened food. He and his own family didn't have a lot, but they had more than most and so he'd shared what they had. But slave labor?

Slaves! His wife, Jutta, was going to blow her top. He was frightened, Audrey had thrown the word death out there like it was nothing important. Like these people's lives didn't matter. Like it was easy to snuff out a life, just like that, with a word.

He walked over to his horse. He'd had to ride the animal to town, it was the only way to get anywhere these days. He was a good horse, about fifteen years old, and didn't mind taking a long ride. He had three other horses that his family rode, and several that they used on the farm.

He'd been using those horses to help with the heavy work. It wasn't enough, he needed more hands. He had three other men working for him, but they could only do so much. Even their families had pitched in. It came down to man power and he just didn't have it. But to have people enslaved, slaves working on his land?

Oh, his wife was gonna throw a fit, he just knew it!

☐

Wilber and Alan walked along the quiet road, lined with large oaks and pines. They had left out after breakfast, it felt like a good day to walk. Wilber liked walking; it kept his joints lubricated. In winter, he stayed indoors, so now was the time to take advantage of the great outdoors. It would take a couple hours to reach Boney's place, so Wilber had filled a poke with some canned ravioli, the kind that had the pop-top, some animal crackers and a few bottles of water and four soft drinks.

They'd seen a few people as they walked, and he'd nod to them. He had an old colt 45 tucked in his waist, his shirt loose and hiding it. He'd made Alan leave the shotgun at home.

"If them KKK boys sees us with weapons, they're gonna take them. Can't have that," Wilber said.

They came to a stop in front of an old gray shack home, it was old but immaculate and orderly. A woman and three children were out in the yard, pulling weeds from a garden. There wasn't a lot there, but the plants looked healthy and seemed to be growing well. The children were neat and clean and looked fit.

He nodded to her, "Ma'am, how be it? Are y'all doin okay?" he asked kindly, smiling.

She stood up and wiped the sweat from her brow. "Bout well as can be expected. Husband's out huntin'."

"Anybody come by wanting your guns? Or some of your food?" he asked.

"No, none so far," she said, suspicion entering her eyes. Her gaze narrowed, looking him over.

"Well, those KKK boys might be paying you and yours a visit. Mayor's send 'em out looking for guns n food. Maybe, you might want ta hide what weapons you have, and leave out the bad ones. Maybe, hide most of your food, only leave out some rotten stuff," he suggested softly. Wilber noticed her eyes soften, a grateful smile curving her lips, she nodded.

"Thank ya kindly sir, I'll tell my husband, when he comes back," she said, smiling once more. Some of her teeth were missing, but it didn't detract from her old-time beauty.

Wilber waved goodbye and he and Alan continued. He knew Audrey would take from even the poorest. A couple of miles down the highway, he and Alan stopped by a heavily shaded curve in the road. The sun was high and though clouds came and went; the sun was beating down hard. Wilber took out a bandana and wiped at his face. He found a wood fence and sat down on the railing.

He surveyed their surroundings but saw no one, nor any animals. The fence abutted a pasture and he wondered if there were any cows. He cocked his head and listened, but heard nothing but the birds in the trees and the constant droning of insects, cicadas murmuring their pleasure.

"You think that family will make it Pop Pop?" Alan asked worriedly.

"I suspect they will, I think they'd been living rough and lean all they're lives. This ain't nothing new to them. The young'uns looked good and healthy and they was clean. Them parents see that the kids grow up right. Now if the mayor will just keep his paws off their food," Wilber said, and sighed heavily as he drank the water.

"Look, someone's comin', on a horse," Alan said, standing up and putting his bony hand over his eyes to shade them.

Wilber looked up the road and saw a thin man riding their way. The man road loosely on the horse, his body in tune with the mount. It took a few minutes for the horse to reach them. Wilber recognized Gerhard Friedhof, he was old John

Friedhof's son, both men were farmers. Gerhard had taken over when his father John, had a stroke.

"Hey Gerhard, how ya doin son?" Wilber asked, smiling up at the man on horseback.

Gerhard slid easily off the horse, his shirt nearly covering his face until he pulled it down into place. Gerhard nodded and his face nearly crumbled in on itself.

"I just done did come from President Audrey's office."

"President?!" both Alan and Wilber said at the same time.

"Yeah, President, and Sheriff Yates is now Vice President. They done made themselves that. I ain't seen no elections," Gerhard said morosely. His hands went into his light brown hair and pulled at it, knocking his hat off. He bent and picked it up and slapped it along his leg.

"You wanna know what they made me do?" he cried out; his nerves seemed to be getting the best of him. Wilber knew Gerhard's father was high strung and it seemed the son had inherited the same nervous energy. Probably why they were so thin.

"What Mr. Gerhard? What they done did?" Alan asked, his eyes wide.

"They made me take slaves, slaves for god sakes. Said I could have them work on my farm or they'd just put them ta death, it was up ta me. All I wanted was some help with getting the harvest on some of the food, so it don't go rotten in the fields. I ain't asked for slaves, sweet Jesus on Christmas," he said and started pulling at his hair.

"What? The Mayor is making you take on slaves? From where and how?" Wilber asked, shocked, but not surprised.

"From the coal mine, said he'd just as soon kill'em. Said was up to me. My Jutta is gonna have a fit, she's just gonna burst a gasket. I don't know how I'm gonna tell her. Oh, she's just gonna be fit to be tied," he said, walking back and forth agitatedly, strangling his hat. He looked to be near tears, his lips trembling.

Wilber looked at Alan and smiled, his grandson blinked. He watched Gerhard's agitated and jerky movements. Then he stood, and placed a calming hand on Gerhard's thin shoulder; he could feel the wiry muscle beneath, like a spring coiled way too tight. Wilber thought the man might fall apart, all his arms and legs going in different directions.

"Gerhard, Gerhard, listen. Son, stop moving and listen to me. This is good. This is very good," Wilber said, smiling.

"Good? Is you crazed man, sorry. It's just that, my Jutta is gonna go irrational on me. Y'all just don't know, her great, great granny was half black. She got cousins in Lexington that is black.

Slaves for gosh sakes. My god, she'll just explode," Gerhard said, near tears, his lower lip trembling.

"Gerhard, sit down, you're about to fall apart. Sit and listen ta me. Me and my friends is lookin for a way ta get them people outta that coal mine. Ta help them escape. Boy, don't you know? We just found that way, with you." Wilber laughed and looked at Alan who had begun to grin, the smile stretching across his thin face, and the light coming back into his sad eyes.

"Do what?" Gerhard asked, his large blue-gray eyes going back and forth between Alan and Wilber.

"Look, it's important ta get them people outta that mine and get them ta your farm. We'll come up with some kinda plan to help all of them folks there ta escape. For now, go along with Audrey, let your wife know it is just for show. If you trust your workers, let them know. We'll figure out something," Wilber said and patted the younger man on the shoulder again.

"Lord a mercy, I just don't want my wife ta go crazy on me. I can't have no slaves, that ain't right. That mayor and sheriff are plum crazy. They scare me ta death, they talked like killen them folks was as easy as blowing out a candle," Gerhard said, snapping his fingers for emphases.

"Yep, well, we'll figure out how to deal with those idjits," Wilber said.

"Thank you, Mr. Wilber, I sure do appreciate your help. I know my wife woulda just lost her mind," Gerhard said and shook Wilber's hand almost violently.

Wilber watched as the man got back into the saddle and set off at a faster pace. The sound of the horse's hoofs clacked off in rhythmic canter. He watched for a long moment and then turned to Alan smiling.

"Well grandson, let's get ta Boney's place, we got some planning to do." He laughed and picked up the bag of food and drink, his step a little lighter.

There was hope, it would be hard, maybe impossible, but it was a chance. It was a better chance than what they had this morning when they'd started out. He shook his head once more at the thought of the crazy bastards that had taken charge of the town. Clearly, they were out of their minds.

If they only knew how many men and women were on the mayor's side, it would help. There would be no clear way of knowing unless they asked everyone, and that wasn't an option, not if they wanted to keep their scalps. Wilber was pretty sure they'd end up in the coal mine themselves. He couldn't blame Gerhard, when

Jutta was riled, she was a force of nature. No one wanted to get in the path of that. He'd heard rumors about her, and shivered.

CHAPTER FOUR

Hobo sat chained to the chair, he'd tried to free himself to no avail. He rubbed his skin raw beneath the chains. He could barely move and his body screamed from pain, both from the drug and alcohol withdrawals he was feeling and also the discomfort of being held in one position. His bones ached and his spine howled, and there was no escaping it. Sleep was fleeting, and he had nothing but dark time on his hands, *or hand or do I even have any hands* he wondered.

He could feel his naked butt, raw from shitting into the bucket below. His flaccid rump sagged through the hole that had been cut in the seat of the oak chair. The jagged edges of the chair's seat now cut into his rump; he'd not been able to lift himself out of the hole. He could smell his own waste, which had mostly been diarrhea. Between that and the cold dampness of the basement, he constantly shivered, irritating his raw skin and his rump.

The old bitch had even taped his penis downward with duct tape and it pulled painfully at the hairs when he tried to shift. She had offered to feed him, but at first, he'd refused and he'd spit at her. The look in her eyes had frightened him, they had nearly turned black. Then the old woman had left him for nearly a week before she came back down, at least it had seemed like a week. He no longer had any concept of time. He didn't know how long he slept or how long he was awake.

It wasn't the same as losing time when he'd been high or drunk. This was so much worse, he had started talking to himself, just to hear something in the dark hole. He listened to his stomach cry, it was hungry and so was making him hungry. He'd called out to her, crying for food and water, but she'd left him there and he was afraid she'd let him die. Then, she'd come down, and she'd fed him. He was glad that he didn't have to eat his own flesh though. He wasn't sure if he could or if that might push him over the edge. The edge was becoming very appealing.

She fed him fruits and vegetables, some of them fresh, some from what she'd said she'd canned. He had to be fed by her hand, and he had to look in her face while she fed him. Her eyes were crazy and when she looked at him, it made his skin crawl. She had started feeding him four small meals a day, bowls of cooked or raw food. She also made him drink lots of water, which made him piss a lot. He could hear it fill the bucket below, and the stench of it floating up to caress his face. At least he wasn't hungry or thirsty any longer.

She came each morning and took the bucket and replaced it with a clean one. Soon, his excrement had become firmer, but it still burned; his butt was chaffed from not being cleaned. When he'd asked her if she were going to clean him, she'd laughed, spit coming out of her mouth and hitting his face.

"I ain't eat'n your asshole, you'll do, you won't die from a nasty butt."

No matter how loud he screamed and pleaded, neither she nor anyone else came to help him. It was dark right now and he didn't know what time it was. She only came down to feed him. He'd awaken some time before, but he'd lost track of time. He wondered if the power had come back on, but no, she had always come down with those lanterns. He wished it would come back on so she could have her freezer back and he could leave. He couldn't remember how he'd gotten there? Had she invited him?

He shifted again and moaned, and then jerked when he heard the door above open. He saw the illumination of her lantern and heard her coming downstairs. He watched as she walked over to the table and place a bundle on it. He saw that she had an apron on, one with dancing chickens on it. She also had her sleeves rolled up above her elbows and he wondered at it. She set her lantern down and opened another solar lantern and the room became brighter.

She turned and went back upstairs and came back a few minutes later with a pot; he could hear the water sloshing in it. He caught the scent of raw potatoes, carrots and onions. She walked carefully over to the table and sat the pot down. Under her arm, she had a shiny metal bowl. He saw her reach for some of her spices she kept down there and he sighed. She was going to feed him. But she usually just brought him down a bowl of something. He'd not seen her do this before and it made him nervous.

She turned around and smiled at him, her smile bright. He began to tremble. That smile meant no good, he was sure.

"What do you want? Why is you here? Where's my vittles? Is that my food?" he asked, his voice quivering and cracking. It seemed to echo in the basement, mocking him, he could hear his own fear. He had to swallow, his mouth going dry.

"Well Hobo, it's time for me to do a little harvesting. I'm sorry to say I don't have anything to numb you with, so this is gonna sting," she said, though her smile didn't diminish.

"No, no. You can't do this. Don't do this Karma, don't," he cried, his breath coming in painful pants.

She laughed hard, bending over at the waist. She laughed long and the tears rolled down her cheeks; she wiped at them with her wrists. She leaned back and hooted and stomped a foot. She shook her head, looking at him.

"My name is Bella May, son," she said and laughed, clearing her throat. She used her wrist to wipe the tears from her eyes.

"I thought you said it were Karma?" Hobo asked, not understanding.

"You know, if I had any doubts before, they are all cleared up. The world will not miss you Hobo dear. Not one whit," she giggled.

She turned away from him and went to the bundle she'd laid on the table and brought back a small clean rag. He began to ask what that was for when she shoved it into his mouth. She reached behind him and her hand came back with a roll of duct tape. She pulled a length and put it over his gagged mouth. He tried to avoid the tape, but her hands were fast and firm.

"Sorry about that, but you're gonna be too loud, and even my ear plugs won't keep the noise out. At least this way, I can enjoy myself without the loud noise," she said grinning, her yellow teeth winking in the light of the lantern. She drew a wooden stool over and placed near him.

His eyes bulged out as she laid out a knife, scalpel, clamps and a small saw. He shook his

69

head wildly. He tried to rock his body, but the chains held him secure. She began to blur as his eyes filled with tears of fear and denial. He tried to scream no, but the rag was blocking him.

His screams were muffled and he shook his head. His body shook with terror, though the movement was very slight and rubbed his rump against the jagged seat. He didn't feel the pain, for the fear that was curling up through his gut and was biting into his brain.

He watched the old woman walk back to the table and she grabbed the shiny metal bowl and came back and placed it on the wooden stool and moved the stool under his confined hand. He screamed and screamed but it was nearly inaudible. His eyes rolled around the room, looking for some kind of escape; he could feel hot tears splash down on his naked chest. His body was vibrating violently with fear and knowledge that pain was coming his way. He could feel himself voiding, he could hear and smell it and he wanted to retch.

"I can't say this won't hurt a bit, cause it's gonna hurt like hell. Most of the time, I don't worry about it, cause my meat is already dead," she said and sniggered, her green eyes bright.

She pulled another stool over and then sat in front of him. She grasped his hand and Hobo tried to avoid her, but he was tightly bound. He couldn't look away as she picked up the small scalpel. He looked at her face and then the dancing chicken apron and then the scalpel. It just didn't make sense to him. She took the blade and cut across his wrist. She held it firmly over the bowl. He watched the blood well up, but there was no pain at first and then he felt the burn and screamed into the rag in his mouth.

He didn't want to watch as the blood spurted from his wrist, some hitting the dancing chickens, some hitting her forearms. She picked up the clamps and clamped something that made the squirting blood stop. Most of it dripped into the metal bowl she'd set on a wooden stool, below his hand. He could feel himself voiding once more when she brought the small saw up and began to saw the bone. His scream went higher as the pain sent white hot razor blades into his brain and then he was gone.

□

David walked among the people in the shadowy mine, there was very little light. They'd not received the requested extra candles, and they'd been told that they had to make do with what they had. He was looking for that new man, Robby Rob. He knew in his gut that the scumbag had stolen food from Mary, and it would seem from a few of the children as well. He knew he should be shocked, but he wasn't.

Gideon Elliot and Steven Stroh, a Beattyville policeman, were helping him look for Robby Rob. Stroh had been put in the coal mine because he had vehemently disagreed with the sheriff and mayor. Especially over the murder of a fellow officer, Howard Deets. They were trying to track down the elusive man who'd been stealing out of the mouths of babes. Robby Rob disappeared and no one had seen him. It was difficult finding anyone or anything in the dusty darkness. There were dozens of shafts and holes and grottos and so spread out, a man could easily elude detection.

The three men met back up near the entrance; it was getting close to supper and they knew Robby Rob would show his face then. David went to check on Mary. He bent and asked if she was okay.

"Yes, I'm fine. I think I need to walk around; my body hurts from sitting in one place," she said, struggling to get up from the pile of covers.

David took her hand and arm and gently lifted her and held onto her while she gained her balance.

"I think I should walk more; I think it isn't good for me to just lay around all the time," she said.

"Just make sure you have Julia or Mary Lou, or one of the other women with you. You don't need to fall, there are a lot of open shafts, old

72

ones. You'll also want to stay near the entrance, that is about the safest place," he advised her. With Robby Rob down here, he knew the man was a predator, and David knew the women were in danger of assault.

He and Mary walked around the cathedral like cavern. David made sure to keep the light in sight, not wanting to get near any of the darkened recesses. There were plenty of trip hazards. He walked her around for about ten minutes, and he watched as she stretched her body. She was trying to work the kinks out.

"Maybe every few hours, have Julia and her boys help you out, get you up and going. That should help with the aches. Get your muscles moving."

"All right David, thank you, I will," she said and he led her around, his arm supporting her back. They walked in circles around other people and children. There were candle stubs spread out, but it was little help.

David walked her back to her pallet and helped her sit down. "Thank you, David, I don't know what I'd do without you," she said, her voice quivering a little. He saw her wipe at her face, moving the mask over her mouth and nose.

"I've told you before Mary, we are all we have here. We have to take care of each other until we get out of here. You don't need to thank me," he said softly, smiling though he could barely see her.

He heard the squeak and squeal of gears, "That's dinner, I'll be back with something and we can sit and have a nice meal together."

She laughed. "It almost sounds normal."

"Yeah, I'm sad to say that it does," David said and laughed.

He walked back to the entrance and waited with others as the platform worked its way down. There were two men, who sported bandanas masking the lower part of their faces. They carried guns and they accompanied the food down and everyone grew silent, waiting to see what would happen. David knew it didn't bode well if men with guns showed up. He wondered at the bandanas, was it to keep their cowardly faces hidden or to keep the coal dust out of their lungs?

"All right, listen up. There's a need for people ta work in the fields. Got some crops coming near to harvesting. Some of the women and some of the men will come with us tomorrow. Y'all can figure it out, but we'll need about fifteen. If you work on the farm, you'll a get ta bring back some of the food," the man said loudly.

"Oh, so we gonna be slave field hands?" a man shouted in the back. David thought it sounded like Robby Rob. He bumped Gideon and nudged Stroh and they slowly shifted backward a fraction.

"Shut the fuck up, boy," the man yelled and pushed the food cart off the lift. The gears began to scream and David turned away, saw Julia and asked her to take Mary food. He then started looking for the man, from the voice that had given a hint of its location. It had come from near C shaft. He tapped Gideon on the shoulder and nudged Stroh and nodded his head. The men worked their way through the throng, and David saw a tall thin shadow, and picked up his pace.

David saw the shape turn and go into one of the shafts, and he and Gideon turned on the lamps on their hard hats. Stroh brought up the rear. They saw a light go on ahead of them and they picked up their pace, nearly running. They had to keep low so they wouldn't smack their heads on the low ceiling, especially David; he was six inches taller than the other two men.

They wove in and out of corridors and dead ends, and had to backtrack. They could hear the footsteps running ahead and then they stopped. It echoed along with their own steps and gave no help in the hunt. David and Gideon slowed and walked as silently as they could, Stroh was wheezing but held his hand over his face. David tried to shallow his breath, but he was winded. He turned his head this way and that, listening for some kind of clue.

Then he heard the scraping of boot on rock and nudged Gideon who heard it as well. They walked slowly forward, their lights moving back and forth over the cave walls. Stroh stayed behind, his wheezing becoming worse and turning into a cough. David heard Stroh back up and away from them. Up ahead they saw an opening and David turned off his light and went ahead of Gideon. His large body blocked most of Gideon's light. He crept up to the low opening and waited for Gideon to come closer.

Just as he suspected, Robby Rob was hiding deeper within the opening. David's mouth turned down when he saw the tell-tale paper towel of stolen food. As Gideon drew abreast and shined his light into the hole, Robby Rob bolted out. David easily caught the man by his scrawny neck. Stroh came running up, sweat running rivers down his face, streaking it with the coal dust.

"Let go man, le…le...let me go!" Robby Rob choked out, spittle flying from his mouth. His yellow eyes rolled around, looking for an escape.

"You little thieving bastard, steal from children and pregnant women, will you? You aren't worth the oxygen you breathe," David snarled, his face close to Robby Rob. He shook the man like a rag doll, Rob's legs dragging the ground.

"I was hungry, those women and young'uns ain't doing nothing. I'm a man, I need that food more than they does," Robby Rob whined.

David began to walk, his pace fast and he could hear Gideon and Stroh trying to keep up. Robby Rob clawed at David's massive hand but it did no good. David's viselike grip would not loosen.

David turned down another shaft and came to an opening that had been boarded up and painted red. David kicked the boards down and Gideon ran up, putting his hand on David's shoulders.

"David, what are you gonna do?" he asked, breathless.

"I'm going to put this asshole where he can't do anyone any harm. I plan to go and work on that farm, to bring Mary back food. I can't protect her with this animal roaming around," David snarled.

"Don't ddd...doon't throw me down there!" Robby Rob screamed, his legs kicking wildly. His hands were trying to hit David's face.

"David, I understand your anger. But you drop him down there, that's just plain murder," Gideon said, his voice hushed and trembling.

"With him, it isn't murder Gideon, I know this peckerwood, he's a bad'un. If you turn your back, he'd stab you and rape your wife," Stroh said, his voice still holding a wheezing note.

77

David looked at Gideon. "Before this all went down, I would agree. I would have wholeheartedly agreed with you. I'd never think of doing anything remotely like this. But Gideon, this is a predator, and he will hurt, kill or even rape those he wants or whoever gets in his way. Letting him live, that is waiting for someone else to get hurt or killed. Can you live with yourself if that happens?" David asked, his voice deadly calm now.

Gideon looked at him, then at Stroh, and then he looked at the ground. David continued, "I will live with the guilt or whatever comes, but I cannot let this man loose around those women and children."

Before Gideon or Robby Rob could say anything, David gave a mighty shove and let go of the man's throat. Robby Rob rocked violently on the edge of the precipice and screamed, his arms windmilling wildly. His face twisted in a mask of fear and horror. Gideon stepped forward to grasp the man's arm, but David blocked his way. Stroh reached out and held Gideon's arm and Robby Rob fell back, his scream echoing down the deep open shaft.

They heard a couple meaty thumps before the screaming stopped and they didn't hear a landing; the hole was deep. David stared into the hole for a few moments and then turned to Gideon, whose face was white as a sheet, all the blood drained. Stroh had his filthy hand on Gideon's shoulder.

"You okay Gideon?" David asked softly, his gaze searching.

Gideon cleared his throat, then answered. "Yeah, David. I'm okay, I guess you're right. It's just…" Gideon stammered.

"I know, it's just not how we are, we don't do the things these assholes do so easily. But we have to Gideon. If we want to get out of here, get our loved ones out of here, then we'll have to change. We will have to become stronger and more ruthless to those who want to harm us."

"Don't waste your pity on him Gideon. Though we could never prove it, he'd hurt a lot of young girls and women over the years. He'd have hurt my wife, yours, and Mary as well as the children. Don't weep for that bastard," Stroh said, and coughed, his eyes burning bright.

Harry and Earl drove slowly around town, they searched the streets. Many of the vehicles had been moved out of the way, making navigating easier. Harry was surprised to see that most of the stores were still intact. There were men and women with weapons in front guarding the buildings and structures.

They were watched, but no one made a move toward their truck, Harry could feel their eyes burning into him. Earl carried the AR-15 across his lap, he also had a homemade vest, with several magazines tucked into it. Harry had his Glock, his hand resting lightly over it.

"Seems like all is pretty quiet. I guess maybe everybody's afraid ta come out," Earl said, his head swiveling around, trying to look everywhere and at everything at once.

"I guess the people know what happens if they cross the KKK, they get put down in the coal mine to work. To become slaves. Or get their heads blown off," Harry growled, his lips thinning as he saw people ahead, very thin. *Looks like the KKK are keeping most of the food for themselves and letting the citizens do with whatever they can scrape together*, he thought, then said, "these folks look like the mayor isn't sharing very much of the food surplus."

He slowed down and pulled up to the group, and they looked at him, fear in their eyes. Harry wasn't surprised, it was fearful times. It both angered him and saddened him.

"Afternoon folks, y'all know where we can find the mayor?" Harry asked cordially, his face neutral.

"You better not let him hear you call him mayor; he is president now. Him and Yates is vice president. When you see them, you have to stop and bow or their goons will beat the crap out of you," a man about forty said, looking sideways at a younger man who sported two black eyes.

"What in tarnation? That sounds just like a dictatorship. Holy hell, that ain't right," Earl said, anger lacing his voice, his face turning bright red.

"Keep your voice down, you can't be bad mouthing the president, my neighbor's grandson was shot, he was only nineteen. Those Nazi boys killed him, for flipping the president the middle finger," a thin woman said, fear written all over her face as she looked around nervously.

"Thank you for the information, I hope it gets better. Is there any place you can go?" Harry asked kindly.

"This is our home, we'll do the best we can, just make sure you stay outta *his* way," said the older man.

Harry pulled away and drove a little farther, then did a U-turn. "I've seen enough, let's get back home. We've got to come up with a viable plan with the least amount of collateral damage. It looks like Audrey has much bigger plans. He is killing indiscriminately, and he isn't feeding these people."

"Baby Jesus love us, that feller is crazy. Shooting a kid, just for being a kid," Earl said, staring out his window.

They turned down a street and saw that there was a roadblock. "Shit, we need to turn around," Harry said and slowed down to make a turn.

"Looks like they're comin' to us," Earl said nervously, his hand fiddling with the AR-15.

Harry stopped the truck and backed up, turned a little then began to back up a little more to turn the vehicle back the other way. A shot rang out and Harry looked back over his shoulder. Men were shouting for them to stop and pull over. They were to be searched.

"No way," Harry said and drew up his weapon holding it ready. He straightened the truck out and began to pull away when another shot rang out, this time hitting the back bumper.

"Give them something to think about Earl, will you?" Harry asked, speeding up, as Earl shifted and pointed the AR-15 out of the window and popped off a few rounds. Harry saw the men scatter, ducking for cover. He saw them through the rearview and smiled. There was no return fire until they'd reached a safer distance.

Once he got to the corner, he turned right and sped away. He didn't want to get into a car chase, he didn't have the gas for it. He also didn't want those men to get close enough to see their faces or the plate on the vehicle. It was time to get out of Dodge.

They passed the group of people and waved, then turned down another street, and Harry zig zagged through the town. He pulled over at one point and both men sat and listened. They heard nothing. Harry pulled out and headed toward the highway. Both he and Earl kept their heads on a swivel, their gazes intent on any kind of movement.

"You think them boys is gonna follow?" Earl asked, searching back over his shoulder.

"I doubt it, we shot back with a high-powered weapon. If they're smart, they'll stay put, if not, I guess we'll see," Harry said and checked his rearview mirror again. He'd not seen any pursuit at all and began to breathe easier. Then a rusted red truck came from a side street. There was an explosion in front of the truck, as asphalt flew up. Harry looked over and saw the truck with three men inside.

"Guess they aren't smart," he said and raised his Glock. "Aim for the driver and spray that cab," Harry said and shot his weapon. The truck jerked this way and that, and the red truck's windshield shattered. Earl kept shooting, following the path of the vehicle. Harry watched and kept a tight grip on the steering wheel, trying to keep from wrecking his truck. The shooting had stopped as fast as it had started and Harry stopped his truck and both men looked back.

The driver was missing his head, blood and brain splattered all over the inside of the truck cab. One man was laying on the ground in front of the truck. He was still moving, but covered with blood and glass. The third man was alive and was trying to get out of the red truck. Harry got out of his truck and began walking toward the men.

"Shouldn't we get goin?" Earl called softly, panic evident in his voice.

Harry walked to the man crawling on the ground and raised his weapon and shot the man in the head. Brain and bone painted the asphalt. Then he looked over to the man, still alive in the destroyed truck cab and lifted his weapon. The man was screaming something and Harry double tapped and the man screamed no more. Harry stood for a moment and looked around and listened.

He walked back to the truck and looked at Earl who was opened mouthed and pale. "Three less assholes we have to worry about. Three less that will be looking for us. We can't let them tell anyone who we are Earl," Harry explained, his voice calm.

"I just... well, I just don't know Harry. I guess I just gotta get used to it," he said and shrugged helplessly.

"I know Earl, it isn't hard to figure out, it has now come to the circumstances that it is us or them. I vote us. If you don't kill them now, you'll have to worry about them later," Harry said and turned his truck toward home.

☐

Boney Patterson sat in his rocking chair, smoking his pipe. Ralph and Abram, the Edison twins were in rockers as well. They'd come for a visit and he was telling them about Wilber's visit.

"The KKK got a new president, that peckerwood, Audrey. I also heard that if ya don't bow down, you'll get the tar kicked out of ya," Boney snorted in disgust.

"I heard tell, they're gonna use them folks in the coal mines for slave labor in the fields," Ralph said, shaking his head sadly.

"That is a good thing, boys," Boney said, laughing as he scratched at his whiskered cheek.

At their identical surprised looks, he sniggered, like a naughty boy, his face folding in on itself with laughter.

"Wilber ran into Gerhard Friedhof; he said that mayor gave Friedhof a choice, either use them people in the mine for slave labor, or he'd kill them. It was Gerhard's choice." He nodded at the double gasp from the twins.

"Some choice. His wife's gonna be mad," they said at the same time.

"Good news, we now got access ta them people. We can coordinate with Gerhard. In the

85

meantime, I am plannin' a little target practice on them peckerwood goons," Boney said, and laughed, rocking back and forth, his old hands gripped his knobby knees in glee.

The twins grinned at each other. "Can we come too?" Abram asked, his eyes filled with glee, Ralph nodding excitedly.

"Well shore nuff boys, we gonna bag us some assholes." Boney laughed again, smacking his knee and rocked side to side and stomped his booted feet. He wiped the tears from his eyes with a knotted and veiny hand.

"Y'all boys go get some of the other fellers, except Hoover, he ain't feeling well. He's getting old," Boney instructed.

Ralph snorted. "He be younger 'n you."

The seventy-seven-year-old twins giggled at that, elbowing each other and Boney narrowed his eyes. He harrumphed and ignored them.

"Tell all the boys, we is going huntin' tomorrow night," Boney said and sat back and puffed his pipe. The aromatic smoke wreathed around his grizzled head. He watched the twin's antics and rolled his old eyes. He needed to take his long gun out and clean her up good. He felt the thrill begin to sing in his veins. His old heart picked up a beat and the years peeled away from him. It had been a long time since he'd shot a

man. He wondered if it'd have the same thrill. He
hoped so.

CHAPTER FIVE

Gerhard stood next to Jutta, his wife of twenty years. She was a tall woman, over six foot two in stocking feet. She had broad hips from having three sons and two daughters. Her long corn silk hair was fashioned into a braid, wrapped at the top of her head like a crown. She stood majestically by her husband, who for once, was moderately calm.

Jutta had that effect on her high-strung husband, her calm demeanor translated to a more serene Gerhard. He'd known her all his life and had loved her just as long. They were twin spirits, and he'd never love another. She looked to him, like a blonde Viking queen, statuesque and strong. She was stronger than most men he knew.

She had a temper, something awful to see, yet she'd never turned her anger on her husband or children. She loved them all with a ferocity and was a good and loyal friend. However, anyone who dared to step between her and what she wanted, they were begging to be ravaged by her wrath. Once she got going, Jutta was like a runaway locomotive mixed with a mad bull; she was nearly unstoppable.

He'd told her about the president and she'd scoffed and laughed. "That jackass couldn't govern his way outta a paper bag."

He'd agreed, but then he'd told her the ultimatum that Audrey had given him and her eyes became hard blue sapphires, sparkling with a simmering rage. He hurried on to tell her about Wilber and their plan to use the people from the mines to help set them all free.

The deep cerulean blue cooled and lightened, anger melting away and she smiled.

"Oh, I'd love to be a fly on that wall, when that scalawag done finds out, he's underestimated his citizens," she said.

They stood with their farmhands, who'd been told to be cooperative with Audrey's people because they didn't want trouble.

"But neither will we abuse those poor people either," Jutta warned, and received the quick and ready agreement. The farmhands had learned never to cross her.

They looked up the road and heard the rumble of an engine, and saw an old beat up and rusted out olive green bus driving down the dirt road. Smoke was billowing out the tail pipe. It sputtered and rattled, but it got to the farm in short order. Two armed men jumped off the bus and began to bark orders. People began to disembark from the bus and Jutta sucked in her breath. Gerhard looked at his wife and then the people coming off the bus.

The people were wretched, covered from head to toe with the coal dust; their thin blackened faces were showing signs of deprivation. He saw his wife begin to expand, and he knew this was not a good sign, but he knew better than to interfere. He saw one of the guards jerk a woman off the bus and she fell heavily to her knees.

His wife left his side and walked over to the man with the shotgun, and she stopped in front of him. He was a few inches shorter and about forty pounds lighter. Jutta grabbed the man by his brown and green checkered shirt and began to shake the hell out of him with her massive hands. Her voice loud and strident, coming out as a vicious roar.

"You're on *my* land now, these people are *my* responsibility now. You got that mister?" she snarled and shook the man harder, her deep blue eyes glittering. The other guard, and the bus driver watched on, stunned, staring open mouthed at the spectacle. The unfortunate man's teeth clacked and his head rocked back and forth violently. She set him down and leaned in, her face so close that her nose brushed his.

"What's your name?" she hissed.

"Bill Hawkins. Ah, ma'am," he said, his voice cracking and his body shaking.

"Bill, I see y'all abuse these poor people again, an I'll skin you alive. You got me? You understand what I'm sayin?" she snarled in a low deadly voice.

The man was shaking and simply nodded and when she looked to the other guard, he nodded as well, his head moving rapidly, his eyes large with fear. Her gaze tracked over to the bus driver, the old man nodded as well. Gerhard smiled internally; he loved his Jutta, she had a good heart and a gentle soul until they opened that bear's cage.

He'd once seen her break a woman's arm for striking one of their daughters. Jutta had beat the woman bloody. No charges were pressed, because the other woman had been in the wrong. She'd never gotten near Jutta or any of his children again. He hoped the man listened; Jutta never made threats, only promises.

She turned to him and he smiled lovingly at her, then she turned to the people. "I'm going to set some hot water out, some soap and towels. I want y'all ta get washed up as best y'all can." She turned to the farm hands. "Get to the store room an get some coveralls for all these folks, they can't work in them nasty clothes. Then I'm gonna make a proper breakfast," she said and turned toward the house. Gerhard knew everyone would jump to her orders, and they did.

He followed her into the house and went up to her and hugged her. He laid his head on her ample breast and breathed, "I love you so much gal, you were magnificent out there."

Jutta hugged him back and kissed his forehead. "We'll make sure all them people are fed and clean. That bastard Audrey will burn for this. My old granny would turn over in her grave if she saw this mess," she said, and sniffed, only showing him the tears. He knew it had broken her heart to see those people treated so badly. He patted her ample butt and hugged her again.

"I'll go out an make sure everyone's getting nice an clean. I'll have them boys tote out the water," he said and left his wife to her cooking; his youngest daughter joined her mother.

☐

Harry sat on the porch, drinking his coffee. Everyone was up early these days, no matter what watch they had. When the sun came up, everyone rose. He'd informed everyone about more changes that had come in town the night before.

Everyone had been incensed about the shooting of the teen. They'd all speculated as to where all the food was going, since it was clear it wasn't going to the people of the town. Also, the armed patrols, sounded like they were trying to disarm the citizens and rob them for whatever they had. Clearly, being in town was now a danger.

Everyone chose to eat their breakfast on the porch. There were small folding tables scattered across the porch. Plates and coffee cups stacked on some, a basket of warm biscuits on another.

"I'm just glad you got away without them following you back," Willene said, sipping her coffee. She'd made oatmeal and eggs for everyone, along with the biscuits. There was butter along with canned peaches that sat in small dishes. Willene and Marilyn made bread, but it was still rising and would be baked that evening. They were using the outside oven. It was harder to bake, but Willene was pretty good at it. He and Peapot had enjoyed her homemade bread, even if there were burnt spots.

"It was a close thing; I made sure that no one followed," Harry said and looked at Earl who nodded. They'd not told the women about the men Harry killed. Clay and Boggy were told, but Harry didn't think the women would appreciate that information. He knew they could handle it, but once more, it wasn't a burden he wanted them to carry.

"I'm taking the guys on a little walk after breakfast," Harry said to Willene and she nodded. He'd spoken to her earlier about taking the men to the cave. She'd already shown Katie and Marilyn, and he wanted to take the men there. If anything happened, they'd all know where it was located and could get there quickly in an emergency.

"Where is we going?" Boggy asked, with a mouth full of eggs.

Harry grinned. "It's a surprise."

"Oh, I like me some surprises," Earl said, his ears pink, a large grin on his face.

Clay stood up suddenly and pointed down the road. There was a group of people walking. From where they sat, they could see there were ten of them, mostly men, a couple of women, and no children.

"Willene, go to my room and set up the Weatherby; you'll have good aim from there," Harry said. Marilyn picked up Angela and called Monroe to her. "Take them into the basement Marilyn, I'll let you know when it is all clear," Harry said.

Clay and Boggy checked their weapons and Earl said he was going to get his hunting rifle. He left the shotgun on the porch. Katie sat quietly, holding her hand gun. Harry smiled at her.

"It should be okay, but their group is a large number. Hopefully they will just pass."

He didn't think so, they were on foot and could clearly see the house from that distance. Had it been night, they'd have missed the house. They had done a few drills and everyone knew their station. They had played out different scenarios. There was just no way to predict what would happen.

He checked his weapon and waited. He brought up the binoculars, the group was still pretty far away. Earl came back to the porch and looked out of a pair of binoculars he'd found. Both men stood on the porch, scoping the oncoming humanity.

"What do ya think?" Earl asked, a cigarette hanging off his lip as he spoke and it bounced, causing ash to fall.

"Not sure, they look rough. Looks like some of the men are carrying hunting rifles. I see one has an ax, another has a baseball bat," Harry said and handed the binoculars to Clay, who brought them up and observed.

"Not sure, those women don't look like they're under duress, they aren't tied up or anything. I think the tall thin woman has a knife at her hip, here, take a look," Clay said and handed the binos back.

Harry looked again, and saw that Clay was correct. They all looked dirty and he figured that was to be expected. Access to clean water wasn't too difficult, but soap and clean clothing might be. Food would be upper most in their minds, not cleanliness.

"Should we at least give them something?" Katie asked softly.

Harry shook his head. "We can't, this is just the first wave, the beginning. There'll be more to come. If people know we have food to share, they'll simply camp out and keep coming back. And then when we cut them off, they'll just come and take it."

"I hate to say he's right Katie, I've seen it before, in the bigger city. People will try to get what they can, and when they can't get it honestly, then they take without regard for those they take from," Clay said.

"Dr. Katie, don't you fret, those men is capable of hunting. But you'll see they ain't done nothing, cause they ain't got no pokes, no bottles. Nothing," Earl said, looking through his binos.

Harry looked again, he realized Earl was right. These people carried nothing, no water bottles, no change of clothing, no backpacks. No one was dragging a cart or wagon. He wondered at that.

"Maybe they just take over a place until there ain't no more, then move on," Boggy said, as though reading his mind.

"I think you hit the nail on the head Boggy. I think they are like locusts, going from one house to the next, eating everything and then moving on. They don't need to carry anything, they eat and destroy wherever they stop," Harry said, his lips pressed down, knowing that this was going to be a fight.

He turned to Katie. "I want you to get into the tree line, about halfway down the yard. There is a big granite rock about ten feet into the trees, get behind that. Shoot anything that tries to come up past you, but stay down." He watched her get up and leave the porch.

He turned to Boggy. "Go get up into the tree blind, pick them off, but stay covered, don't get shot, and pick your target carefully, don't waste a shot."

Boggy took off, going down the hill and into the woods to the left. They had spent an afternoon putting up tree blinds, elevated spots where they could shoot from and protect the house. So far, they'd manage three blinds, though one was yet to be completed. It afforded them the ability to hide and shoot from the woods.

Earl walked off the porch and headed down the hill. Harry and Earl had dug a hole down near the middle of the hill, with Monroe's help and had made a kind of foxhole. With heavy boards, they had removed Willene's car door and had put it against the boards, and put the dirt in front of the door, so it looked like a dirt hill. Earl could shoot from that position and stay relatively safe, between the heavy dirt, wood boards and metal of the car door. They had talked about more, spread

97

out on the property. Now they would see how this position worked.

Clay stayed with Harry and both men waited quietly. They watched as the group got closer and they could see them talking excitedly among themselves and pointing up to the house. It took nearly ten minutes for the group to come to the barricade. A rough looking man, big and burly, though clearly thinner than he was normally, his clothes bagging on him. He seemed to be their leader or spokesman, because he came forward.

"Hey, y'all got any food and water to spar?" he shouted.

Harry shouted back "no" and waited, he and Clay watching them talk amongst themselves. He didn't want to engage them anymore than he had to. He wanted them to know that they were not welcome.

"That ain't very neighborly mister, we're hungry," the man shouted back.

"We aren't your neighbor and you need to move along, now," Harry said loudly, his voice devoid of emotion.

One man from the group began to move through the blockade and a shot rang out, the dirt exploding right in front of the man who'd stuck his head through the hedge. He jerked back, and the others in the group scattered, ducking down and hiding.

"Why did ya fire at us, we were just gonna talk," the man called, anger lacing his voice.

"I told you to leave. I have shooters with their weapons aimed at you. They see you step foot on this property, they'll shoot to kill. You've been warned," Harry called down to them and waited to see what they'd do. To show weakness to these people meant death.

Another shot rang out and a man screamed, he fell out of the woods about ten feet up onto Harry's property. He'd been trying to come through the woods, the young man, Boggy, had shot him. A smile creased Harry's lips.

"You shot our man!" someone screamed.

"I warned you. If you don't pull yourself off my property mister, I'll kill you now," Harry yelled down to the man who was stumbling up, holding his bloody arm. The man looked up the hill at Harry. Harry brought his Glock up and aimed it at the man on his property.

The man hastily staggered to the barricade and hands appeared and pulled him through. Clay and Harry stood silently on the porch, and then they saw the group leaving, passing farther up the road. Harry counted to make sure all ten were leaving. They were. He let his breath out and went to sit on the swing. He shook his head, and knew this was just the beginning.

"Can you tell Marilyn to bring the kids back up Clay, if you don't mind, I think my legs won't let me stand," he said and laughed.

"I know what you mean, my legs feel like they got water in them. My adrenaline is pumping overtime. That was close, but I think we did well, we had a good plan, and everyone did their part," Clay said and patted Harry on the back and disappeared into the house.

"Come on back everyone," Harry called, though not too loudly. A few minutes later, Boggy came out, grinning. Then Katie came out of the woods, much of the color leached from her face, but she was walking firmly.

Marilyn and Willene came out on the porch, Willene holding Angela, who she then let down to play on the porch. Angela toddled over to her wooden blocks and stuffed animal and sat and played. Monroe went over and sat down beside the small child. Willene watched her for a moment and then sat down. She looked at Harry and grinned.

"Good shooting sis, I'm proud of you," Harry said and grinned. She blushed but was happy. She took a deep drink of her cooling coffee.

"I sure hope they don't come back," Marilyn said, her eyes large and filled with fright.

"They shouldn't, they've already seen shots from multiple positions, so they don't know how many people we have. But they do know we are well armed. They'll go for easier pickings," Harry assured her.

"I just hope they don't attack the dairy," Willene worried.

"They are pretty well armed there, Earl and I stopped over to check on them. Their farm hands and their families have moved in and seems like they have it together," Harry said.

"I think we did well, everyone was on top of it," Clay said.

"I think that was just the first of many," Katie said, her teeth nibbling on her bottom lip, worry in her dark eyes.

"I think you're right bout that. They'll be like fleas on a hound dog soon," Boggy said, wiping the sweat from his face. Harry thought he looked a little pale, but otherwise fine. It was a hard thing to shoot at another person. He suspected this was Boggy's first and he suspected it would be even harder when the young man had to actually kill someone.

"Let's go for a walk gentleman, Willy, if you need me, send Katie to get us. We'll be back fast," Harry said and got up, his legs a bit stronger.

"No worries brother, got this covered," she said and smiled. Harry laughed when he saw Earl's face flushed with excitement, apparently Earl *did* like surprises.

Harry led the way up the back of the property, past the garden, chicken lot, corn cribs and into the woods. All the men were quiet, Harry thought they were more than likely wondering what was going on. He took them the most direct route to the cave, ten minutes later he came to the large cluster of boulders and rocks. Everyone was looking around the area, then back to Harry with questioning looks. Harry grinned and reached over and pulled the bushes aside, revealing a narrow fissure opening.

"What in tarnation?" Earl said and grinned widely, his eyes as round as saucers.

Harry turned on his flashlight and led the group of men in; they were silent behind him. He could see behind him; that someone had turned on their flashlight. And he heard Earl giggle, like a kid who'd just discovered that there was a Santa Claus. He smiled, and led the way down the steps into the main chamber of the cave. He walked over to a lantern and pulled out his lighter and lit it.

Clay whistled long and low, his head turning this way and that, shining his flashlight around the large room.

"Now this is the coolest mancave I've ever seen!" Clay said laughing and smacked Harry on the back. Harry grinned at him.

"This is the damnedest and the greatest thing that I ever did see!" Earl cried in an excited voice, his gaze darting and searching and the biggest smile that Harry had ever seen. Boggy looked around stunned, his large eyes taking in everything, but he was silent, his mouth shaped in a silent "O".

"My family has had this cave for many generations. Me and Willy played here as kids and did our own decorating. Recently, my grandfather made some modifications and he has also saved our lives. Follow me," Harry said, and he led the way.

He lit another lantern and gave it to Clay, and Harry carried one as well. They stopped at Harry's room and Earl giggled again. His eyes crinkling into deep triangles of humor and hilarity.

Clay sniggered and picked up the action figure and looked at Harry. Harry grinned and shrugged.

"This is wild, man, I wish I'd had some place like this when I was a kid." Clay laughed and picked up a comic book and flipped through it.

"Jeezum, this is great!" Earl said in wonder, his head on a swivel.

Boggy followed behind with a huge smile on his lips, his gaze caressing over each item. For Harry, it was like seeing the cave anew. Through their eyes, and he had to admit, it was pretty damned awesome.

With each room, they stopped and everyone had a look around. They didn't touch Harry's mother's things and were reverent and quiet, even Earl had calmed down.

"This is amazing Harry, I really mean it. I know it is a cave, but it really doesn't feel like it. It isn't cold or dank or anything," Clay said, his voice filled with awe.

"This is amazing," Boggy said simply.

"I could live here an be happy I figure," Earl said, sighing with a kind of bliss.

Harry laughed. "We loved it as children, but we'd been warned to keep it a secret all our lives. It has been a place of refuge and safety in the past. If something happens and we have to bug out from the farmhouse, we have this place to come to. All I ask is that you never tell a soul. Only us, our family," Harry said softly. The men stood in a small circle and looked at each other smiling and nodded to Harry.

"We promise Harry, for our family only," Clay said.

Harry took them to the vast storage cavern and he heard Earl choke and snigger at the same time and he looked back at him. Tears were sliding down his face and he was shaking his head.

"Your Peapot did this Harry?" Earl asked, wiping the tears away. Harry knew how Earl felt, with all the supplies here, they could live and survive.

"Yeah, I didn't even know it. I don't know how long he'd been working at it. Remember, I told you he said that he knew the coronal event was coming. When I first saw it, it nearly knocked the breath out of me," he explained, going farther into the room.

"I guess your grandpa loved y'all a lot, you and your sister," Boggy said softly, his eyes looking around at all the neatly stacked boxes.

"He did Boggy, he sure did. I also think he knew that I'd be having friends come to stay as well." He smiled at Earl and Clay, who grinned back at him.

Boggy walked over to Harry and hugged him, and Harry heard Boggy sniffle. Boggy pulled back, tears in his eyes.

"I ain't had no one to care about me but my granny, but now I know y'all all care bout me. I'm humbled about it, and I thank ye," Boggy said, swallowing hard. Harry felt the sting of tears in his own eyes and reached out and hugged Boggy to him, patting the young man on the back.

"We're all we have in this world Boggy, and I figure God got us all together for a reason, my

Peapot just made it so we could live a little easier, and have enough."

They walked through the rest of the cave and Earl liked the kitchen and bent over and took a drink from the natural sink. He looked up and grinned happily.

"That is some good water. Cold and fresh," he said grinning foolishly as he wiped the moisture from his mouth.

"Well, if something bad happens, that we can't live up at the farm house, I expect we'll do just fine here Harry," Clay said.

They all left the cave and began walking back to the house, taking a different route.

"Me and Willy are careful coming up here, in case anyone is around, and especially now. We come and go in different directions. Because of so many rock formations on the property, I'm hoping it will confuse anyone who is following."

"Good idea," Clay said, he was carrying a box of supplies, some coffee and sugar. Earl was carrying a twenty-pound bag of beans, and Boggy had two large boxes of powdered milk. Harry carried a large sack of flour. Willene had sent him with a list of needs. Harry figured they could all carry something back.

No one spoke on the way back to the farmhouse, everyone listening intently. They saw Brian and Charley playing in the back of the house with Monroe and Marilyn was in the garden with a basket gathering ripened vegetables. Much had been canned already, and this was for their dinner later that evening.

Harry drew in a deep breath; he felt peaceful knowing he had his friends and family around him. With a little luck and planning, they could survive this, if they could keep the hordes at bay. He knew in the coming weeks and months, it would become harder. More people would die at their hands. It was the them or us mentality. If Harry could feed them all he would. But that was an impossibility. The sad fact was, many were going to starve to death.

Alan drove slowly; ahead of him was a truck, loaded with something boxy beneath a tarp. He recognized the truck; it had a large confederate flag painted on the tailgate. It was Mr. Andy Anderson, and Alan knew the old man was part of the KKK. He wondered what the old man had in the back of the truck. He kept his distance, he didn't see anyone else in the truck but he didn't want the old tyrant to identify him. Andy was a mean old man, always had been. His grandfather had warned Alan away from the old geezer.

Alan never knew why the old man was so hateful. He'd not liked blacks at all and would spit on the ground when he passed one. There were altercations and yelling matches. Most folks knew to steer clear.

He saw that the truck's brake lights kept flashing. Alan wondered if the old man was riding his breaks. They were heading down a slope, but it wasn't steep. He slowed his own truck down and looked around him. There were no other homes or buildings near. They were on a deserted stretch of road. He wondered if the man was trying to trick him. It wasn't difficult to see him from behind.

Then he watched as the truck sped up and careened sideways and hit a tree, the hood of the truck popping up. Alan slowed down, waited and watched to see what the old man would do. Nothing happened. The old man didn't get out of his truck. Slowly, Alan pulled his truck near. His eyes going to his mirrors and looking around. He didn't think it was a trap. He didn't see anyone or any other vehicles.

He pulled abreast to the cab of the truck and saw that Andy was slumped over, he wasn't wearing a seatbelt. He put his own truck in park and exited, leaving his truck running. He went to the window and looked in. Andy's eyes were wide open and his mouth was as well, as though he were silently screaming. Reaching an arm through the open window, he poked at the old man hard.

"Mr. Anderson? Mr. Anderson, is you okay?"

Nothing, no movement nor could Alan see any chest movements coming from the man. He shoved harder at the old man, but Anderson didn't blink, didn't move. Around him the road was silent, he heard blue jays crying in the trees and the cicada's soft murmurs.

Must have had a heart attack, Alan thought. He walked to the back of the truck and untied the tarp. Stacked in the back of the truck bed were boxes and boxes of food. Alan's legs nearly gave out, there was a hell of a lot of food. He wondered if Mr. Anderson was taking it to the KKK. He also wondered if the man had stolen it from hungry people, and his brows furrowed down.

A slow smile spread over Alan's homely face. He unloaded the boxes of food, transferring them to his own truck. His heart was racing since he knew someone might come by and he sure didn't want to get caught taking the food. He kept a look out and it only took ten minutes to finish. Next, he untied the rest of the tarp and spread it over his own truck, covering his prize. He walked back to the cab and looked in. He saw a shotgun, leaving it. Someone would eventually find Mr. Anderson, and he didn't want anyone looking for a gun thief.

He wondered if this man was responsible for the murder of his friend. Rage roiled up within him. He placed his bony hands on the open window of the driver's side door. There were no answers from this man and Alan was glad the old goat was dead. One less target as Harry would say.

He hopped back into his truck and gave a final salute to the dead man and drove quickly away. He'd find out who needed food and start giving it away. He smiled then sniggered at the thought of besting the KKK and the mayor. He would hide the bulk of the food in Dr. Katie's burned-out home. No one would think of looking there. Most of the structure was down, but there were a couple rooms that were safe from the elements.

He laughed out loud and smacked the steering wheel happily. This was a stroke of luck, and maybe a stroke for Mr. Anderson, he sniggered, his eyes triangles in humor. It was the first true smile he'd smiled in a long while.

CHAPTER SIX

Boney, Wilber, the Edison twins, Sherman Collins and Thornton Sherman stood in the middle of a deserted road. They were roughly about a mile from town. They had left their vehicles two miles away. Boney had caught a ride from Wilber. They had all walked the two miles in. Boney listened to the joints popping and old bones creaking for the last two miles. He'd wondered when they'd all gotten so old? Soon, they would go their separate ways, to hunt their targets.

The thought of the hunt once more sent a thrill through Boney's old body. He felt the old dusty adrenaline begin to warm and flow through his veins.

"We ain't gonna hit that coal mine, things are in play and we don't wanna skunk that up. Only pick one target tonight. Make sure you kill'em an get the hell out of there," Boney instructed, his face covered with black, it was wood ash and boot polish. He wished he'd had his old camo kit, but that had turned to dust decades ago.

The rest of the old men had varying camouflage, leaves and branches stuck to them, from head to toe. They resembled old withered trees. Boney smiled, *we may be old, but it don't take much ta pull a trigger.*

111

The men separated and went into the forest or along the road. Boney walked purposefully. He was going to kill the bastard who'd tried to kill his cousin, Clay. He'd heard through the grape vine about some peckerwood who'd bragged they'd killed a black cop on the highway from Lexington. Boney knew from Wilber, that Clay was alive. He had a bone to pick with that jackass. *The idjit should have known better, there was always kin somewhere to avenge,* Boney thought.

Whitney Porter was his name, and he lived out in some beat down trailer park. He'd wanted to take a vehicle, but it would be seen for miles and this was a black op. His gait was slow but steady; he took the time to take in his surroundings. He'd lived in this town his whole life, except for when he'd been sent to Vietnam.

It had been his first venture out of these hills. He'd gone to Lexington a few times, but he'd never had that big a desire to leave his home. He'd been drafted into that far away war. He'd been selected when they found out what a crack shot he was. Boney had numerous kills under his belt. He prided himself on clean shots and single shots. He still hunted, though he only used his hunting rifle for that.

Times had changed and when he'd come home, people at the airport had tried to spit on him. One look into his deadly eyes and their spit dried in their mouths. His eyes told them that he'd kill them quick and easy. A prey knows when it sees a predator. Those idiots knew not to screw with him. A soft wrinkled smile of remembrance creased his old face.

It took him over an hour to get to the park, and he'd made his way quietly through darkened trailers. He didn't hear any dogs, figured the poor folks had already eaten them and their cats. He felt sad for the children. This was going to be a hard world for them to live in. He hoped that their folks did their best to feed them.

The street lamps were out; there was only the sky and that provided little light. Boney didn't need much light, his old eyes had adapted to the darkness. The homes were quiet around him, curtains drawn tight. He could almost smell the fear in this place. He couldn't blame them.

There was a swastika painted boldly outside of Porter's trailer, he wasn't very subtle about it. Boney stood for a moment, it was quiet, everyone asleep. He had to get the little shit out of his trailer. He thought for a few moments. He looked around him and saw an old plastic orange gas can. He walked over and picked it up. There wasn't much in it as he shook it, but, he didn't need a lot.

He crept over to Porter's trailer and picked up multiple pieces of garbage that were strewn around his small yard. Most were empty beer packages, and those made of cardboard. He heaped them under the door and along the side of the trailer. He sprinkled the little bit of gas that was left in the canister and left it there with the debris. He pulled out his old and worn Zippo lighter, he'd had it since Vietnam. He lit the edge of a large cardboard box, holding the lighter in place until it caught, then he backed up some distance from the trailer. His keen eyes scanning as he went. He hadn't noticed anyone looking through their windows. All was quiet and still.

The trash was slow to fire, and he wondered if it was too damp, but as the fire worked its way along and the gas caught, the fire grew bigger. Soon, it caught onto the underside trailer, *the insulation maybe or exposed wood*, Boney thought. He found a place that had a clear line of sight and no obstructions, and set up his rifle. He was roughly four hundred feet away, an easy shot. He lined up his rifle's sights, and waited patiently. If the idiot slept through it, then he'd just be a crispy critter. But Boney really was wanting to put a bullet through the asshole's eye, he wanted to make a point.

He watched as the blaze grew, and Boney could see that the interior had ignited, he could see flames dancing and licking its fiery tongue through the filthy windows, white curtains lifted by the heat. Then he saw a figure, moving, in a crouch. His old heart leapt with joy and once more he could feel his adrenaline swim through his veins, singing that siren's song. He took a deep breath, *slow is smooth, smooth is fast*. He saw the door open, a man, illuminated by the fire stood looking around, his hair sticking straight up from sleep and filth. He had checkered shorts that sagged around his narrow hips and he had a grimy wifebeater undershirt on that was stretched over his gut. He stepped down, barefooted, from the doorway. With a gentle caress, Boney pulled the trigger and felt the thrill as the butt of the rifle gave him a love tap.

Whitney Porter's head exploded; though Boney had aimed for the eye, the high caliber bullet took Whitney's head off completely. Brains and blood and skull fragments peppered the shell of the trailer and swastika. He normally made his kills from farther out. *I guess that will make a statement*, Boney laughed to himself as he got up from the ground, his old bones and joints protesting by popping loudly, like dried branches. He turned away from the scene and walked the long walk home.

He could hear people screaming behind him, but he was so far away from the trailer, no one looked in his direction. He paused and turned and watched for a few moments. The people were gathered in front of the dead man's trailer and

Boney could no longer see the headless man. Once more a smile creased his face. It was a sweet smile of remembrance. He longed for those days gone by. He'd wasted his youth with being young. Youth truly was wasted on the young and he chuckled at that.

The fire from the trailer helped illuminate his way for a while until he turned at a bend in the road. He heard an explosion and a wide smile split his withered face. He snorted and shook his head. This was the most fun he'd had in years. He didn't feel the aches and pains that plagued him constantly. He was sure the adrenaline rush had taken care of that.

It was darker now and he slowed his pace. Then he heard a shot ring out in the distance. Someone found a target and he tittered to himself. Ahead, he saw lights of a vehicle heading toward him. Easily, he slipped quietly into the bushes and waited. It wasn't long before an old truck rumbled past him, he waited for a few moments, until he could no longer see the tail lights.

He waited and listened for more vehicles but heard none and then stepped back out onto the road. He heard another shot, this time closer. It was all working according to his well-designed plan. Back in the Revolutionary War, there were tactics like theirs. Go in and hit the enemy and then disappear. You couldn't catch what you couldn't see. He sighed heavily in pleasure.

He kept up his meandering pace and ten minutes later, he heard rustling in the trees; he paused and waited. He heard the harsh breathing of someone, he thought it was Thornton, so he pulled out his pipe and lit it and waited. The old Marine came out of the trees, grinning like a fool.

"That sure was fun," he said, laughing in a whisper, and started coughing. He wiped the sweat from his brow and shook his head.

"I've not felt like that in a coon's age. Gad, it was sure fun, an' man oh man, that ol boy didn't know what hit him. He and another feller were just standing there shootin' the shit, smoking. When I dropped that little bastard, the other near shit himself tryin' to get away. I wanted to kill him too, almost did. Maybe next time I will."

Boney laughed, it had been a long time since any of them felt this alive. He could still feel the adrenaline flowing in his veins like sweet honey. He drew on his pipe and patted the younger man on the shoulders. They walked in companionable silence for a while. The air around them had become damp and the clouds were beginning to gather for an argument.

"Looks like it might rain," Thornton said softly, his voice sounded like water on gravel.

117

Boney sniffed the air. "Yep, but it'll be nigh on morning until it gets here," he said.

They heard the low call of a mourning dove. Then they heard twigs snapping and the Edison twins materialized. Both their heads tilted the same way, their shoulders hunched. They were such carbon copies of the other, it was spooky at times. Both men were wearing disappointment on their identical faces. Boney figured they'd not found a target. He was right when Ralph complained, "Couldn't find nobody, can't tell who is who in the dark."

"Next time, choose a target ahead of time, that'll be easy nuff, just listen to them pecker-heads in town. There's a lot of braggin bunches of jackasses." Boney laughed. This perked both brothers up and they nodded happily.

"When can we go again?" Thornton asked hopefully, his eyes glistened in the low light of the night.

"I'd say let's give it a week. Let their guard down," Boney said, letting a plume of smoke out. The crickets had resumed their chorus and silence settled over the group. Each man was in his own thoughts. Boney felt very satisfied with himself. The only problem he could see was who to choose next, there were so many worthy candidates.

He hoped that Wilber had gotten himself a target. The man had parked his truck a few miles away and would make it home by himself. It had been a successful foray and Boney felt elated. One less bastard in the world. He wished he could see the mayor's pudgy little face when he found out. His shoulders shook in silent laughter at the thought. He'd seen the little bastard throw a temper tantrum or two in his time. He shook his head and wondered who'd voted the jackass into office.

One by one, his companions left him, turning down a road to either their truck or their home. Boney was alone now; he'd wanted to walk the rest of the way home. He was sure that Wilber would understand. A man needed to be alone with his thoughts sometimes. It had been a good night. He was well satisfied with the men and the mission.

By the time he reached home he was tired, his old body wasn't used to that much walking. He'd walked the hills around his home for hours, but this had been different. He stopped in the kitchen to grab an apple and munched it on his way to bed. He could see the pale fingers of dawn through the windows, though it would be an hour or better before the sun showed its face. He felt deeply satisfied and it had been a long time since he'd felt that kind of satisfaction. He felt a sense of pride and usefulness. Getting old wasn't for the faint hearted. But this adventure had made him feel young. It was a damned good feeling.

☐

David helped Mary to rise from her pallet, he was taking her to the farm. He'd spoken to Jutta about her, and the woman had urged him to bring Mary; she'd said she'd handle things on her end. They walked toward the platform as people gathered. They were also taking two small children with them.

David and Gideon had discussed it with Gerhard, they were going to smuggle out the smallest children first, one or two at a time. The small children could hide within the group of people heading to the farm to work. Today there would be eleven people going to the farm. Mary stood in front of David, his massive hands resting on her shoulders. Two children were sandwiched between them.

He and Mary and the children stepped onto the platform along with several other adults. They began to feel the platform shiver and shift and the cables groaned and the platform began to rise slowly. David could feel Mary trembling and he squeezed her shoulders. He could also feel the two boys and their trembling. He knew the children were afraid and the boys cried, leaving their parents. Their parents cried as well, but had told their children to go. His eyes had teared up watching the farewell. These children were fragile and they needed out of the coal mine.

The platform jerked hard and David heard the boys squeal softly. His large hand settled on the children and squeezed them lightly. He hushed them gently and told them it was okay. They were getting off the platform.

David found out that they'd been down in that hole, a little over a month, he knew that made Mary nearly six months pregnant. It had seemed a lot longer and the morning light hurt his eyes. He held a hand up and shielded himself, his eyes squinting.

Jutta had let them bathe, and it was the first time he'd felt clean in a long time. She'd also fixed them all a big breakfast, bacon, eggs, biscuits and gravy with sliced tomatoes. Nothing had ever tasted so good. He wanted that for Mary, he wanted her out of the hell hole.

Her shoulders felt bony and when he got a good look at her in the morning light, he nearly wept. He blinked furiously, she was so thin, and her belly protruding, but he thought, not as big as it should have been. Her dark hair was matted to her head, thickly coated with coal dust. He looked down at the children between them and they too were covered heavily in the oily dust. He wished he could get his hands on the mayor and sheriff.

They were herded onto the bus, the guards not even looking into their faces. The two guards that had been with them the first time to the farm were there. They had the good graces to look ashamed of themselves. He noticed that they'd covered up their swastika tattoos, which they'd previously flaunted. David was sure the men saw the children, for they looked away, their heads hung in heavy shame. He saw the bus driver's lips tremble and he too looked away.

The bus ride to the farm was quiet, no one spoke and the children were kept low in the back seats, sitting between Mary and David, their huge eyes filled with fear. David had to blink back tears, they were covered in thick oily coal dust, and they were wretchedly thin. Their small hands twined into his big hands and he smiled down at them gently and squeezed their hands. They grinned, and settled back down, one looked up with a set of bright blue eyes and the other dark brown eyes. Both children were nearly jet black, so covered in the thick mess.

The bus arrived twenty minutes later and everyone began to disembark. Jutta and Gerhard were standing there waiting for them, along with their older boys, Seth, Jeb, and Leon. All were tall young men, the eldest seventeen. David thought they favored their mother, though they had their father's wiry strength.

Mary was in front of him, and the children still between. The three boys moved in and took the children quickly away, before the guards noticed, though David knew it wouldn't have mattered. David heard Jutta suck in her breath and he smiled internally; her eyes had become hard and deep cerulean when she'd seen the children and Mary. He waited patiently for the explosion.

"Are you kidding me?" she asked Hawkins, the guard she'd shaken, on the previous visit. He shrank from her, his arms coming up defensively, as she came forward like a locomotive, her arms chugging her along.

"Do you see this pregnant woman; do you see that she is skin and bones? Do you see her?" Jutta roared. The man could only nod quickly, shame stamped heavily on his face and he looked at the ground, his face blossoming into bright red. Jutta swung her eyes to the other guard and then the old driver, who looked down as well.

"By the love of the Lord Jesus Christ, this I swear with my last breath. I will gut you if I hear of you harming another person. I will wait until you aren't expecting it and one day, you will look down and the loops of your intestines will be splattered down at your feet. This woman will stay with me here. She won't go back to that hole. And you will not tell anyone, do I make myself clear?" she hissed in a low deadly voice.

All the men nodded obediently; the color washed away from their faces. David had no doubt whatsoever that they believed her. He'd heard about the fight Jutta had with some woman, and of Jutta beating the hell out of her. It had been the talk of the town. No one doubted it when Jutta promised retribution. She fairly vibrated with outrage; her eyes had nearly gone black and she was breathing heavily. She was so close to Hawkins, that he thought that Hawkins might shit himself with fear. She turned and gently took Mary's arm and led the woman away, and the three guards watched, then looked at each other and shrugged helplessly. Their bodies relaxing as the threat moved away from them.

There was a long table that had been set out for everyone to wash up and they were able to change their clothes. Their own rags would be washed and left to dry in the sun while they worked the fields. It had been good to bring more food back to the rest who'd been left behind to work in the mines. Most of it had been distributed among the children first.

Jutta had also sent cookies back and all had enjoyed that rare treat. Today, there were more women that had come to work in the fields. The men opting to do the heavier work down in the coal mines. Also, this gave their women a chance at good food, a bath and sunshine. All which they'd been denied for well over a month. David heard the women oohing and ahhing over the hot water and heard their splashes. He knew that exquisite feeling of being clean.

David watched the guards surreptitiously; they seemed subdued. He wasn't sure if it was from Jutta's rant or something else. Maybe their white power play wasn't working out how they'd wanted it to. They, too, were looking a little on the thin side and when Jutta had offered them breakfast as well, they'd jumped at the chance, eating ravenously. *Maybe things aren't as equal in the KKK world as you thought it would be,* David thought with a smile. A hungry man was a disgruntled man.

☐

Jutta clucked softly like a worried hen, her throat feeling clogged at seeing the poor children and this pregnant woman. She felt her heart constrict and it conflicted with the rage that swam through her veins like a hungry shark. She felt the heat of rage break like the incoming tide. She wanted to go out and shoot those men, but she knew they were only acting out of fear and orders. She'd seen their shame clear enough; they knew they'd done wrong. She'd also seen how thin and hungry they were as well as the people from the coal mine.

EMP Antediluvian Fear   S.A. Ison

She was sure also, that those men had not missed seeing the children, but had turned a blind eye. Perhaps there was hope for them yet. She hoped so. She had her daughter Milly pour hot water into the tub, it wouldn't be a lot, but at least Mary could sit and bathe in privacy. She'd helped the woman undress and nearly burst into tears when she saw Mary's ribs. Mary's backbone was sharp down her narrow back. Her lips trembled as she tamped down the emotions that threatened to drown her.

She gently wiped Mary down with a clean rag, getting most of the grit off her body before letting her bathe. She left Mary to her bath and went to tend to the two small children. She could feel the tears slide down her face when she quietly closed the door. She leaned back against it. She couldn't stop the tears from falling. Her heart was shattering over and over. She took her apron and wiped at the tears. She shook her head and blinked her eyes, willing the tears away. That poor woman's body was near skeletal. If that baby lived, it would be a miracle.

Trina was helping the two boys wash up in a basin. Their faces slowly becoming clean. She saw they were thin, but not as thin as Mary. She figured their mothers had given them the lion's share of the food. She wished she could get her hands on those bastards; she'd tear them apart with her bare hands. Her knuckles popped loudly and her hands curled into tight fists. She wiped once more at her face and walked over to the boys.

Each child had been given a t-shirt, their own clothes taken away to be washed. She took a soft cloth and lifted each face and wiped the residue away. For now, they were clean enough, but they'd be bathed again later. She was sure it would take a few hot soapy baths to get rid of the grime.

Each boy had a large biscuit with bacon and egg inside and a large glass of fresh milk, from the morning's milking. The boys looked to be four and five, one was black and the other white, though she'd not been able to tell when she'd first seen them. Their hair was matted and filthy, their tiny bodies caked in grime and coal dust. It took numerous washings, but they were close to clean.

Their small hands wrapped around the biscuits and they ate solemnly, their cheeks bulging. Their eyes seemed overly large in their heads. Once more, Jutta had to clamp down on the overwhelming urge to cry. She bit down on her lip and smiled with difficulty down at the boys.

Mary came out of the bathroom, looking better.

"Thank you, Jutta, I feel like a new person," Mary said and smiled shyly. She was wearing a dress from Milly.

Jutta smiled and bit back the tears, blinking rapidly.

"Come and eat Mary, we need to fatten you and that baby up. I have some fresh squeezed milk," she joked and Mary laughed.

Both women sat at the large farmhouse table, and Mary began to eat and sighed heavily as she enjoyed the flaky biscuit. She took a drink of milk and groaned in delight. Jutta smiled, her blue eyes lighting up.

"I'd never thought I would say that eating a biscuit and drinking fresh milk was almost sinful," Mary said.

Jutta laughed until she cried and then Mary started crying and Jutta got up and gathered the shorter woman into her arms and hugged her and held her for a long time. Both women were weeping, rocking back and forth. Their tears wound down and both heaved a very heavy sigh and laughed, wiping the tears away. Jutta reached over and grabbed a couple of tissues out of a box sitting on the counter. She handed one to Mary.

They realized the two small boys were watching them open mouthed and Jutta smiled sweetly. She went over to the boys and picked up each in her arms and sat down holding both in her ample lap. She kissed both their small heads and hugged them to her breast, causing both boys to giggle.

"What's your name boys?" she asked gently, giving them each another biscuit, this time filled with fried apples.

"I'm Jack," said the little black boy.

"Hi Jack, how old are you honey?"

"Oh, I's five," he said, taking a big bite of the biscuit and chewing methodically. Both women smiled and Jutta kissed him again on his head. She jiggled the other little boy, which made him giggle.

"What's your name honey?" she asked the little white boy.

"I's Robert," though he pronounced it, Robret. She jiggled him again and elicited another giggle.

"And how old are you, Robret?" she laughed and he held up four fingers. She kissed his head and Mary reached out and drew the four-year-old to her lap. She kissed his head and held him close to her and laid her cheek on his small round crown. Her hand caressed his thin arm. She handed the boy a biscuit filled with fried apples.

"I truly cannot understand why these people are so hateful. Were they always this way, do you think? And a disaster was the right recipe to make them act like this?" Mary asked, taking another bite of her biscuit, and then another drink of milk.

Jutta shook her head. "Sweetheart, I wish I knew. But if I ever get my hands on that you know

what, I'll end all his problems fast," she said, her
deep sapphire eyes glinting. Mary smiled and
nodded. Jutta felt the child in her lap growing
heavy. His small body sinking into her soft flesh.
She could feel the heat radiating off of him.

Jutta saw that both the boys and Mary looked
near to passing out with a full stomach. She got
up, Jack still in her arms. His body was becoming
limp and she heard the soft snore from him and
smiled.

"Come on Mary, I'll put you and these
young'uns ta bed, you sleep as long as you like.
We got to get you back to fighting weight," she
said and smiled over her shoulder as she led the
way upstairs.

☐

"I want ta know, who in the Sam Hill killed
our people. By god, we ain't gonna stand for it,"
President Audrey shouted, his fist hitting his desk,
his face an alarming red and purple.

Vice President Yates sat quietly watching
Gene Grady making the report. "Sir…"

"That's President Audrey, you will address
me as President Audrey," Rupert shouted.

"Yes s.. President Audrey, the shootings were
done spread out, one guy's head, that was Whitney
Porter we think, got his head blown clean off. We
can't tell for sure," Grady said, swallowing hard,

his eyes darting between Audrey and Yates, a fine sheen of sweat breaking out over his upper lip.

"Another, Mac McBride, he was shot standing guard by the Quick-mart, Larry Town said he'd not seen a soul, that Mac just dropped to the ground. Then there was two volunteers, Jim Striker and Rudy Hoskins. They were shot as well, near on about the same time."

"Looks like someone is picking off our boys," Vice President Yates said slowly, his red hair nearly matching the red in his face. He didn't like this. It was cowardly, he didn't like an enemy to hide. They were spread thin enough without having to worry about some vigilante taking their people out. It didn't help that Audrey wanted a contingent of bodyguards around him at all times.

He snorted, and looked up, realizing he'd laughed and Audrey's face was turning purple. He held up a calming hand and nodded Grady out of the office. Once the door closed, he looked to Audrey.

"Look Rupert," he started.

"President," Audrey said petulantly.

Yates's mouth thinned, his eyes narrowing. "Look Rupert, this is to be expected. There are a lot of people unhappy with us and with our people. This is a surprise only in that it took so long. I figured we'd get much more resistance, so that is a good thing. It has to be expected that there would be people to push back."

"But I'm the damn president and people ought to respect that," Audrey snarled, his small fist clenched, his beady eyes squinting. His lips were pulled back and his yellow teeth shown dully in the office, he had a patchy beard growing. His hair was greasy and flattened to his round head.

"It's only been a month, maybe if we give them a little more food, they'll be a little more compliant. Power through the stomach and all," Yates said rationally.

"But I want," Rupert began.

Yates brought his large fist down on the desk with such force that the papers flew in all directions and Audrey jerked back, nearly falling out of his chair.

"No! Listen here you little fuck, you're the only one that buys your brand of Billy Bob bullshit. You had that fucking kid shot for flipping you the finger. A kid for Christ's sakes, you think those people respect you, you think they will call you president? You'll be lucky you don't get your goddamned head blown off. I don't give a shit that you want to play president, but you keep that shit low keyed. I'm not going to get my head blown off because you don't know how to handle people. You'd better give the goddamned order to distribute more food, or you'll have more deaths

132

and some serious fucking unrest," he snarled angrily, his face beet red and his breath blowing out his nose like a blown horse.

He stood up, gave Audrey a scathing look and turned and walked out of the office, slamming the door so hard, the glass shattered. He didn't look back, because he was a hair's breadth away from shooting the jackass in the head.

Grady was standing out in the hall and gave Yates a look, and Yates shook his head. Both men headed outside and onto the sidewalk. He turned to Grady, his voice much calmer, the bright alarming color receding.

"Look into these shootings. This was a well-coordinated attack, and that means military to me or police. You and Smalls get out there and sniff around and keep the fucking rhetoric down. Give out some food, these goddamned people are starving, especially the families with children. Do it now," Yates ordered. Grady looked at him for a long moment and then nodded.

"They found Andy, his truck hit a tree, but I think he had a heart attack. He was supposed to be bringing some food in, but I don't know if he did or not. There wasn't anything in his truck."

"Was he robbed? You sure it was a heart attack?"

"Yeah, his shotgun was right by his side and he was leaning over sideways, his eyes open and all. No sign of foul play that they could tell."

"Shit, does anyone know where Andy kept the food stored?" Yates asked, biting his bottom lip, thinking.

"No, but I'll head to his house and see what's what."

Yates nodded and looked around the street. It was empty. It was eerie, there was no noise. Even the birds seemed quiet. He felt the hair raise along his neck and his eyes narrowed, scanning the windows of the buildings around him. He felt like he was being watched. He caught a movement in a store across the way, though when he looked, he saw nothing.

"Okay, go ahead and get to it. Watch your back, I got a feeling that things are going to start to get hairy." Danny Yates watched Grady walk away. *How the hell had all this gone sideways* he wondered. It was Audrey and his self-important bullshit. Things were going fine until he named himself fucking president. *What a complete jackass, I should have shot him instead of Deets,* he thought.

He began to walk back to his office, slowly. He didn't want to show fear, but fear he felt. He could feel that primordial fear curling around his shoulders. He could feel eyes burning into his back. It was all he could do not to turn around and look. The world had turned upside down and he was thinking that perhaps raising up the KKK hadn't been the best strategy. It had been Audrey who'd pushed for the killing of the Santo family. Andy had been all for it as well. Yates hadn't raised a fuss, he was all for getting rid of the family, but he'd have been satisfied with putting them in the coal mine or sending them on their way.

Nowadays, when people looked at him, he'd not seen smiles, only blank stares. Some hostile, but quickly hidden. The older people didn't bother hiding their contempt. One old timer had spat a stream of tobacco across his path and when Yates had looked at him, the old bastard stared with hateful eyes, that drilled into Yate's soul. The man had been old, but he was sure that if the man had a gun, he'd have been shot down there in the street.

If life was rough before the end, it was dicey and chancy at best now. He'd have to rethink this thing with Audrey, he was becoming a liability.

☐

Boggy walked along the creek, he had developed a hankering for some fish, and so he'd gathered up a pole and tackle box and headed into the woods. It was quiet out here and he enjoyed the solitude. He knew Harry had a few places to fish and Harry had mentioned the best pond to go to. He took his time, enjoying the quiet. He heard the rustling of the critters that made the forest their home.

He carried Willene's Ruger LC9s 9mm gun in a shoulder holster inside his loose shirt. He'd not wanted the extra weight of his hunting rifle. He was well hidden in the woods. He felt comfortable walking alone. He wanted his hands free for carrying a lot of fish back home. He smiled at the thought. It had been a long time since he'd gone fishing. He enjoyed the idleness of it.

Marilyn packed him a lunch to take with him as well and he whistled softly to himself as he walked along. Monroe wanted to come along, but his mother had made him stay to weed the garden. Boggy grinned, he understood the boy's plight, his own granny made him pull weeds from their garden. She'd said it was honest work and would keep him out of trouble. She'd been right about that and he laughed softly to himself at the memory.

He thought about the cave, he'd never seen so much food and supplies. It reminded him of one of those big stores with racks and racks of food. He couldn't get over the forethought that Harry's grandpa had, and had accomplished. It was truly a miracle and he felt blessed to be a part of their family.

He well and truly cared for each member of the household. From Angela to Harry, they all meant a lot to him. They had all treated him with kindness. One evening, they'd been sitting on the porch. He'd felt the need to talk and he'd revealed to them that he was gay. He'd waited for their condemnation, their anger and repudiation. They had all looked at him and shrugged and smiled.

Then Willene had laughed, a sweet laugh and then, Katie and Marilyn and Harry had followed.

"Boggy, I'm gay too," Willene said and everyone started laughing, including Boggy. They wiped the tears away and Willene had gotten up and hugged him. He'd wept in her arms, he'd never felt so loved and accepted, since his grandmother. Clay and Earl grinned as well and smacked him on the back.

"What's gay?" Monroe had asked and everyone had laughed harder, and Earl had picked the boy up and squeezed him in a hug.

"It means happy," Earl had said.

A soft smile curved Boggy's face when he remembered that night. Boggy came to a small stream, that fed into a larger stream that fed into a good-sized pond. He sat his rod and tackle box down. He stood looking around in the clearing; it was peaceful and the wind blew the bright green leaves around, above him. He could hear squirrels chattering, not happy about his presence. He could also hear the low constant buzzing of the cicadas.

He squatted and dug around in the tackle box for the right fly and affixed his hook and then cast his line into the pond. He sat near the bank and listened to the blue jays that were fighting in an oak tree twenty feet away, he knew it was full of acorns. He heard frogs croaking somewhere in the cattails and heard small splashes. The air was full of soft soothing sounds. He could feel the sun beating down on him.

He was getting sleepy when he felt the first initial tug on the line, and he began to reel in the fish. He felt the tug and pull of the fish that translated up the line and into his arms. He could tell that it was a good-sized fish. He grinned broadly and reeled it in. It was a trout, about thirteen inches long. He knew it would make good eating. He ran a line of paracord through its gills and placed it back in the water. It would stay trapped on the line until Boggy took them home.

He marveled at the thought of *home*. It had truly become his home. His grandmother's trailer had been his home, but once she'd died, he'd felt alone. He no longer felt that way. He felt safe at the farmhouse and he felt welcome and useful. He shuddered to think what his life would have been like had Earl not come to his home to collect him.

He'd never even heard of an EMP, it was something invisible, yet had changed their world irrevocably. He may have lost his old home, but he'd gained a new home and a new family, one that he cared deeply for.

He cast the line out once more and sat down on the grass. He leaned over and pulled a long stem of grass out and put it in his mouth. He began to chew it and tasted the sweet green taste of it. The constant and hypnotic drone of the cicadas lulled him into sleepy contemplation.

His eyes began to grow heavy again until he felt a stinging pain against the side of his head. He fell over, the fishing pole falling to the ground. His eye sight was blurry and his head pounded and he was confused as to what just happened. He blinked rapidly, his brain trying to figure out what was going on.

He looked around and saw two white men standing over him, broad grins on their filthy faces.

"Well look what we have here, a black boy, a fishin' and don't you know he's trespassing on someone's property, probably a white man's land," the greasy blond said and snickered. He had a filthy gray tank top on, that had a decal of a woman, that had nearly been peeled off. His teeth were gray as well and thick with a buildup of

139

scum. Boggy could smell the stench of his breath from the ground.

"It's a good thing I brought me some rope Dale; I think we're gonna have us a good ol fashioned hangin."

The other man laughed; he had dark brown hair that was matted to his head. He had an eyeball tattooed on his throat and a swastika under his left eye.

"You know? I ain't never hanged no body, except for them Mexicans. They did scream lots, especially that boy. It sure was fun and that momma, she was fun before we hanged her," Dale said and laughed, his blue eyes burning down into Boggy's face.

Boggy's heart was beating hard, and fear nearly took him over until he felt the Ruger digging into his armpit. He started crying, to give himself time, but also to grieve for Angela's family. This was the bastard who'd hung them, and he'd also raped Mrs. Santo.

"Oh, this here chicken shit boy is cryin Randy, maybe he done think we're gonna rape him," Dale said laughing and hopped around in glee.

"That don't sound half bad, I ain't had a woman in a long time," Randy said.

"Is you queer? Shit hellfire, boy," Dale said, apparently shocked, his mouth hanging open.

140

"No, I ain't a queer, but you know, ain't nobody's know but us," Randy said turning bright red.

While the two argued back and forth, Boggy slipped his hand, which had been beneath him, into his shirt. He felt the gun and pulled it from the holster. He could feel the blood running from his head. He saw that Dale had a branch, which he'd used as a club. Boggy pulled the gun out and he felt for the safety and slid it off.

He rolled slightly and pulled the gun from beneath him. He shot Dale first in the chest, and Randy screamed and jerked back as warm blood sprayed his face. He was about to turn and Boggy shot him in the side of his chest. Randy went down heavily beside Dale, who was still alive.

Boggy got up, staggered, and then stood, he was still crying. He wiped at the blood and tears that were covering his face. He walked to the two prone men, Randy was gasping, the bullet having entered his lungs but had not exited. There was a large bloody stain growing on his shirt.

"What...what ya go an' do that for?" he said, trying desperately to catch his breath. Boggy brought up the weapon and Randy tried to scream, raising his arm, but Boggy pulled the trigger and unleashed a 9mm and shot the man between the eyes. He walked over to Dale, who lay looking up at him, hate in his eyes. There was blood coming out of the corner of his mouth. Boggy aimed the gun lower, and shot the man between the legs. Dale howled in pain, the dark stain spreading across his crotch and thighs.

"That's for Mrs. Santo and her family," Boggy said in a dead voice. He holstered the gun and stumbled to the pond. He dropped to his knees and brought a handful of water to his face. He closed his eyes as pain washed over him. He felt his gorge rise and he turned and vomited on the grass. He brought a shaking handful of water to his mouth and washed it out and spit the water onto the grass.

He took the hem of his shirt and wiped at his face. There was still blood trickling down. He got up and staggered toward the two downed men. He stooped over and grabbed Randy's feet. He began to pull Randy by his feet; he pulled and tugged, stopping twice to vomit. It took time, but Boggy had pulled the body away from the stream and pond. He didn't want the rotting body to pollute the waters.

He staggered back for Dale, who was still alive and moaning and crying. He walked up to the man, his eyes cold when he looked down at him. He walked around the man and kicked Dale in the crotch, causing Dale to scream, his hands trying to protect his bloody groin. Boggy grabbed him by the feet and began to pull him into the forest, intending to put him by his friend. Dale moaned and cried as Boggy dragged him.

"Ain't you gonna kill me?" Dale cried, his head bouncing up and down on the uneven ground. Boggy didn't answer, he just kept pulling the man. It took nearly twenty minutes. Boggy could feel the sweat pouring off his face, mixed with the blood. His shirt was covered now in blood, soaked. His long legs screamed at the abuse and his head pounded. He hoped he wouldn't black out.

He finally made it to the other body. He sat on a rock for a moment, breathing heavily. He spit out a bit of blood and wiped at the blood and sweat off his face once more with the bottom of his loose shirt. He stared at Dale, the man was still alive. He took out his weapon and aimed it at Dale's midsection, he shot two times and each time Dale screamed.

"I killed you, but you'll take a bit ta die. And I hope that maybe something might come and eat ya afore you do die," Boggy said and grinned down at the man, who could no longer speak, but grasped his belly, pooling with blood. Boggy leaned forward and spit into the man's eyes.

Boggy turned and walked back to the pond, he paused several times, squatting, trying not to vomit. He wiped again at his face. When he got back to the pond, he took out his water and drank it slowly. He sat on the ground and cried. His thin shoulders shook. He'd come so close to death. But he'd lived. And he'd avenged the Santo's family. He took another drink, then forced himself up. He walked to the pond and he let the fish go and packed his gear up and turned for home.

He felt rage and sorrow but he also felt a deep sense of satisfaction on Angela's behalf and that of the Santo's family. He'd avenged them in a small way. He hoped that Dale would live long enough for a bear or coyote to come and gnaw on him a bit before he did die. A savage smile curled on his face. He felt no regret whatsoever.

☐

Mary woke slowly, her eyes blinked open and she wriggled her body around on the soft mattress. She'd never thought she'd feel a mattress again, or breathe clean air, or have clean sheets. Tears welled in her eyes, such simple things, things she'd not even thought of before. She sat up slowly, and placed her hands on her belly. She blinked her eyes and could feel grit in them. She knuckled each eye, knowing it was the blasted coal dust.

It had been the baby to wake her, it was moving around a lot and she was so thankful. She had feared she'd lose the baby down in that hellish hole. She looked around the room, it must be the girl's room, there were two twin beds, with flowered comforters on them. She hadn't really noticed; she was so exhausted when she'd gone up to the room. She'd been asleep before her head hit the pillow.

There were stuffed animals, posters and all the girly girl things that many girls decorated their rooms with. It was a bright room and it made her smile. The memories of the horrible darkness were starting to slide away.

She looked at her hands, they still had coal dust in the creases of her joints and in her nails. She'd seen her face in the mirror and she hadn't even recognized herself. A sob caught in her throat. If David hadn't gotten her out of there, she knew she would have died there. She knew her husband would have liked David a lot. If she had a boy, like they'd said, she'd name him Howard David Deets.

She got up slowly and made her way downstairs. She'd slept almost five hours and it was just after noon. Jutta was in the kitchen, making the afternoon meal for the workers. She smiled at Jutta who reached over with flour covered hands and hugged her.

"Have a seat, there's some fried apple pies on the platter and some more milk." Jutta nodded.

"You sure you don't need help?" Mary asked, taking a seat at the large farm table. The table was heavy oak; its top was nearly satin smooth from years of use. The table was cluttered with a large basket of eggs, a large glass cylinder jar of flour, a pitcher of milk, spices, two chickens that had been plucked and cut up, and a large bowl of string beans, which Trina was snapping. She smiled shyly at Mary.

"The girls are all the help I need; you relax and get stronger. We got this," Jutta said and smiled.

Milly came in with a large basket of potatoes, she came to the table with a sharp knife and sat down. She pulled a large potato out and began to peel skillfully. She too smiled shyly at Mary and Mary returned her smile. The kitchen was bright and airy, with windows that covered one wall. She could see out to the fields and pastures. Jutta turned and poured a cup of coffee and put more milk in it, then she handed it to Mary and grinned.

"There's some coffee with your milk, sugar is in the sugar bowl if you like. I suspect it's been a while."

"Oh, this is nice," Mary cooed softly and sipped the coffee. She hunched her thin shoulders forward and tried to wrap herself around the cup, letting the steam rise into her face. She inhaled sublimely, a soft smile curving her mouth.

Jutta laughed. "Yeah, I love my coffee too, and when I was pregnant, they told me I shouldn't have it, but I drank some with my milk and as you can see, it didn't hurt the babies none." She grinned, nodding at her two daughters, both miniature images of her.

They all laughed softly and everyone got busy with the meal. Mary reached over and took a potato and Jutta gave her a knife. She began to peel, enjoying the simple task. It was quiet but for Jutta's soft humming.

"Where are Jack and Robert?" Mary asked, looking around.

"They're outside playing, I have Leon keeping an eye on them. Figured they could do with some sunshine and play. Fed them up a bit of apple pie and milk as well. That seemed to pep them up," she said laughing. The girls joined in, giggling and looking at each other, the tips of their ears turning pink, like tiny mouse ears, delicately shelled.

The door opened and all women looked over and saw the large form of David. He looked at the women and when his eyes found Mary, his smile broadened. His eyes going to triangles of joy.

"Come on in David, have some coffee," Jutta invited.

David kicked the dust off his boots and stepped into the kitchen. He accepted a cup of coffee which nearly disappeared in his large hand. When she picked up the pitcher of milk, he grinned and shook his head, then took a sip. A low groan emanated from deep within his chest, his eyes closing.

The women tittered and Jutta flushed with pleasure. She handed him an apple pie, the flaky crust perfection. Mary thought he might cry, and he took a bite and stomped his foot and shook his head.

"Jutta, will you marry me?" he asked and all the women burst into laughter, Jutta turning bright red but grinning widely.

"This is wonderful, thank you. I wanted to let you know that we got about thirty more minutes, Gerhard said ta let you know," David said, then took a sip of his coffee.

"That sounds good, lunch should be ready around then," she said, smiling still.

David nodded, he looked at Mary.

"You feeling better Mary? We were really worried about you," David said, his face solemn.

Mary smiled at him. "I'm feeling more human now, than I have in a long time. It feels so good to breathe fresh air and not feel that oily grit all over me."

"Yeah, I'd say you're right on the money with that. I'll head back out. Ladies," he said putting the empty cup on the counter and he nodded and left them.

"He is the sweetest man, I'll swear," Jutta said, blushing. Her daughters giggled and nudged

148

each other and she shot them a look. Mary buried a smile in her coffee cup. She thought that perhaps Jutta had a tiny crush on David. He was indeed a sweet man. She watched him as he headed out of sight.

Once more she didn't know what she would have done without his help and his support. She was sure she'd have sunk into a deep depression. Her mind went to Howard, he'd been gone only a month or so, but it seemed like a lifetime had passed in the coal mine. She shivered and Jutta looked up at her and she smiled, picked up a potato and started peeling once more.

Life was so strange, she'd gone through most of her life in peaceful bliss. Howard had shielded her from a lot of the ugliness in the world. As had her parents. But when she'd been manhandled by the men and thrown into that pit, life became crystal clear. There were good men and there were bad men. She just hoped that the good men outnumbered the bad, or life would be hard and brutal.

CHAPTER SEVEN

Vern Smalls got off his horse; he was going to different houses gathering food supplies. Guns if there were any. He was also looking for the bastards who were shooting up their people. He spat a long stream of dark liquid, a lump of chew in his lip. He stood looking around a moment. Many of the homes were abandoned. From the looks of them, they'd also been looted.

He wondered at the windows that were broken, why break windows? He shook his head and walked up the sidewalk of a prospective home. The grass was becoming overgrown. He didn't hear any children or dogs and wondered at it. He came up to the porch and knocked. He listened and heard movement within. He knocked again, this time drawing his service weapon.

"This is Officer Smalls, from the Beattyville police department. Open your door, I only wish to speak with you."

Slowly, the door opened and a young woman peeked around the door opening. He shoved the door open wider, knocking her back. He stepped into the house, his eyes darting everywhere.

"Why didn't you open it when I knocked the first time?" he asked, annoyed.

"I didn't know who you were," she said.

He scrutinized her up and down and saw two boys, playing in the living room, they looked to be about eight and nine. He looked for her husband, if she had one but didn't see anyone else.

"Where's your husband?"

"We've not seen him since the power went out. He'd been in Lexington and we're hoping he will come home soon," she said, her voice cracking. Vern looked at her closely, she was young and pretty.

"You know anything about the killings that have been going on? Raids against our people?" he asked, watching her eyes.

She shook her head, confused. "No, I don't leave my home, it's too dangerous out there."

"Fine. Fine, I need to confiscate any fire arms you may have. Also, I will need some supplies from your pantry."

"What? You want my food? I don't have much, and I have two small boys. I can't give you any food, I need it for them," she said, her voice beginning to rise.

Vern looked over into the living room, the two boys had stopped playing and looked at their mother, fear in their eyes. He swore under his breath. His knuckle rubbed hard on his upper lip, thinking.

"Well, I'm authorized by the president to take what I need for the town," he said, then looked at the boys once more. He lowered his voice, "however, if we were to, say go back to your bedroom. Maybe send the boys outside to play in the back yard for a time. I might be persuaded to forego the food supplies. I might also be able to stop from time to time to *protect* your home, for the night." There was an oily smile on his face.

The woman looked at him and then to her two children. Tears beginning to well up in her eyes. She cleared her voice several times before she could speak.

"Boys, why don't you two go out and get some fresh air. Go play in the back yard, but don't go any farther. You hear?"

"Yes, ma'am," they said in unison and got up from their toys on the floor. Both boys went out into the back yard and Vern could see them on their swing set. He turned and smiled like a well satisfied crocodile.

"Lead the way my dear," he said and laughed.

She walked ahead of him, he could hear her crying now, louder. It didn't bother him. In fact, he thought perhaps this could be very nice for him. Perhaps there were all kinds of women out there, without their men. They might need his protection as well. He might as well get something for his troubles. After all, he was putting his life on the line, making sure the streets were safe. He chuckled to himself as he began to unbutton his shirt. He closed the door softly behind him. *Yes, this could work out very well*, he thought.

□

Harry had just finished chopping wood. He and Boggy had dropped some trees thirty feet back from the tree line. Boggy had come back from his fishing trip, bloodied and Harry had come across him first. Boggy had wept when he told Harry about the men, especially Dale, who'd raped and hung Mrs. Santo and her family.

Harry had taken Boggy to Willene, and she had put a butterfly bandage on his head after she'd cleaned him up. When he'd told her about the men, she smiled grimly.

"Good, I hope that bastard suffered a mauling from a hungry bear," she'd said. The word passed around their small family and Boggy received hugs and pats on the back. That had been nearly two weeks ago. Harry and Willene kept an eye on the young man. He seemed to be doing better. The first few days he was a little nauseated. Willene and Katie worried that he might have a concussion. He was babied and hugged and seemed to enjoy the attention from the women. Harry smiled. Who didn't like being cared for? Boggy eventually leveled out with his emotions.

Harry noted that Clay and Earl would go and pat Boggy on the back from time to time. The manly equivalent of a hug of reassurance. Harry knew it hadn't been hard to pull the trigger on animals like that, but afterwards, when it was replayed in Boggy's mind, which Harry was sure it did, that was when the real emotions surface.

When your life is in jeopardy, all emotions go to the back, while fight or flight comes to the fore. Boggy had fought for his life, but he'd also had the presence of mind to extract vengeance for the family done so wrong. Harry was proud of the young man. He was also glad that Boggy seemed to be moving past the episode.

Harry was pretty sure that it would happen again and again with the movement of strangers passing by their home. He was surprised that it had been as quiet as it had. He knew that peace wouldn't last long. They had spent a few minutes in the evening, listening in on the shortwave radio, but heard nothing. He'd turn the dial slowly, but so far, he'd picked up no chatter.

He was sure people were on the move now. Time didn't stand still for the hungry and desperate. The ten people who'd come by had only been the first. He was hoping the distance in the mountains would slow the masses down. It had for a time. It was going to be an ever-rolling tide of humanity.

Harry stood for a moment, wiping the sweat from his face. He looked around him. The trees that had been felled would sit there for a year.

They had used the chainsaws, it was the fastest way to bring down the large trees. They had to pause to sharpen the teeth of the chainsaws in between the cutting of several trees.

"Since we're cuttin these trees down, why not cut them into small chunks here and now?" Boggy suggested.

Harry stared at Boggy for a moment and a slow smile spread on his face.

"I don't even know why I didn't think about that. You're right, because come next year or the following, I don't think we'll have gas for the chainsaws. Or at least any useable gas," Harry said, shaking his head. He smacked Boggy on the back, who grinned shyly.

Both men turned the chainsaws to the task of delimbing the trees and the slow process of cutting the massive trunks down to size. It was hard work, and dangerous as well. The kickback from a chainsaw could easily cut off a limb or even slice into torso or face.

The chunks of tree trunk would dry faster and make for easier transporting as well. For now, they would leave most of the tree chunks up in the forest. They worked methodically, choosing trees that were big and some that were dying. They found two large trees that had been downed sometime in the last couple years.

"At least we can use this for this winter," Harry said smiling.

Boggy nodded; he took a drink of water that they'd carried in bottles. They were reusing the bottles from bottled water. There was little wasted or thrown out. It was quiet around them as they took a break. In the distance, they heard the cry of a woodpecker and then they rhythmic drumming on a tree. Harry breathed in deeply.

"It's peaceful here."

"It sure is, I like this place a lot. You got a nice parcel o land," Boggy said, looking around in the forest. They both froze when they heard the gobbling of a tom turkey. Both grinned at each other. Boggy got up slowly and reached for his hunting rifle, his eyebrows waggling. Harry laughed softly and nodded.

He watched as Boggy slipped away into the woods silently. He heard the gobbling once more, this time closer. He waited for a long moment. He knew Boggy was an excellent hunter and turkey on the menu would be nice. Harry liked using what was around them. Dipping into their stores was okay, but harvesting from the land was better.

Once more he heard the bird, and then a shot. He jerked slightly and stood, waiting. He listened, turning his head this way and that. Then he heard branches snapping. Then he saw Boggy's tall form, his rifle up against his shoulder and then saw in his hand the body of the turkey.

Harry gave a shout of laughter, and saw Earl and Clay coming up through the woods. They both had their weapons to the ready and he smiled and waved. They brought their weapons down. Boggy came toward them, raising the turkey and grinning hugely.

"Dang, that's some kind of bird you got, Boggy," Earl said, chuckling and took the bird from Boggy and hoisted it in the air.

"Yeah, it's a heavy boy."

Clay reached over and took the bird from Earl and lifted it experimentally. A broad smile sweeping his face.

"Nice shooting, Boggy," Clay said, and handed the bird to Harry to admire. Harry lifted the bird and cocked his head from side to side.

"I'd say nearly twenty pounds, what do you think Boggy?"

"I'd say, pert-near close to it."

Everyone sat on a large log or chunk of wood to relax a moment and enjoy the momentary quiet. They all grinned at each other like idiots, happy about the turkey.

"I guess I'd better get that bird ta the women, I figure Willene will be mad if she'd don't find out what the shootin was all about," Earl said getting up and grinning as he picked up the heavy bird.

Clay laughed and slapped his back. "Yeah, you know they want to know everything, and I don't want them to worry either, about the shot. Good shooting Boggy and thanks for dinner."

Harry and Boggy watched as the two men disappeared with the bird. Harry sighed and picked up his chainsaw. Boggy did the same. Harry began to cut the dead tree into smaller, more manageable chunks. Once that was done, he and Boggy loaded up an old wagon and Boggy took off toward the house.

Harry knew Earl would begin to split the wood and stack it. Earl had tried to help the day before, but it was difficult for him to walk in the woods with his prosthetic leg. Boggy would deliver the dead wood and come back for another load. Harry turned to the next large log and began to cut that down. He was glad for the downed trees, they would need it for cooking now since there were more people to feed and also for laundry and heating in the winter.

It was hard and heavy work, with only their hands. Harry was glad that the chainsaws worked. He had plenty of gas and figured he'd cut down a few more trees than was necessary. He didn't know how long the chainsaws would last nor the gas to run them. Cutting a tree down by ax was a daunting thought.

He and Boggy had cut ten trees the day before. They'd cut them into six-foot sections. But he would go back with Boggy's idea and cut them down further. Boggy came back through the woods and smiled as he loaded the wagon and departed. Harry kept the chainsaw going.

They'd now cut nearly twenty trees, large hardwoods. The trees, and their wood, would last them for some years, years after the chainsaw would be useless. At first Boggy didn't understand why they were downing so many trees. But when Harry mentioned about the loss of the chainsaws in a year or two, Boggy agreed. Now, with Boggy's suggestion about cutting the trees into smaller chunks, it was a better solution.

"That is some far ahead thinkin, and I got a feeling it'll save us a lot of hard labor," he said.

"Work smarter, not harder my Peapot use to say," Harry said, wiping the sweat from his face. It was a hot day, but he could tell the nights were starting to get cooler. If they used their resources wisely, they could live comfortably for many years to come, even with all the extra people.

He thought that perhaps tomorrow, they would cut down more trees. The more he thought about it, the more he hated the idea of having to chop down trees with an ax. Then cutting the tree into smaller chunks and so on. He knew it was the old way of doing it, but he didn't think he'd actually want to do it that way if he could help it. Plus, if the men were incapable of cutting down the trees later, the women would be hard pressed as well.

Willene could cut wood with the best of them. But as they all aged, their strength and infirmaries would hinder them. He was trying to think ahead. Boggy was the only really young man there. Katie was young, but she was a tiny woman and he doubted she'd have the ability to fell a tree.

He was used to everyone now, and it seemed odd that they'd not been there all along. He thought fleetingly of his Fran, but pulled away from the thought, he'd never see her again, and he'd moved on. He was surprised that everyone got along as well as they did. Their personalities seemed to mesh well. Everyone worked hard to make it work, to ensure all chores got done, all watches taken, so everyone was able to sleep soundly and safely.

Time was passing fast, and he'd not heard from Alan. He hoped the boy was okay. He thought about going and finding the boy, but he didn't want to draw attention to him, it had not gone well their last trip to town. He was also low on gas; and if he planned another trip, they'd have to siphon more gas, he could get it from Willene's car and Marilyn's car. He hoped the kid could make it back soon.

He knew that Willene and Katie were in the kitchen canning green beans they'd picked earlier this morning. Marilyn had babysitting duty, and she was snapping the beans. Now they had a turkey to pluck, or perhaps Clay or Earl would take over that duty.

Clay was roaming, keeping watch, he'd seen him earlier, before the turkey shoot, making his rounds with Brian and Charley at his heels. He knew Earl was back to chopping wood, and he could hear they rhythmic thump of the ax. He saw Boggy once more and smiled. He helped load the wagon once more with the heavy logs. He and Boggy made their way to the wood pile pulling the heavily loaded wagon behind. They unloaded the wagon and tossed the logs into a pile awaiting the ax.

Earl stopped and took off his bandana and wiped his face grinning.

"I guess we'll have plenty of wood for the winter," he said, leaning on the long ax handle.

"Yeah, we dropped quite a few trees and sectioned them up. I don't know how long this old chainsaw will last, maybe longer than the gas," Harry said. He heard the women laughing from the house and smiled. He also heard Monroe squealing and laughing.

Earl smiled. "Yonder little man wanted ta help me. Hated ta send him on, bless his little heart. Now I expect he wants to help with the turkey."

"Sounds like he's giving Charley and Brian a run for their money. I guess the dogs didn't go with Clay, deciding Monroe was more fun than patrolling," Harry said, he could now hear both dogs barking at the child who was squealing in reply.

Boggy brought him the dipper from the well bucket. It was cold sweet water and he drank, enjoying the cold feeling of it going down his throat. He walked over and dipped another scoop full and drank it down. He dipped again and brought it to Earl who gratefully took it and drank.

"That is some good water," he said, smacking his lips.

"Let's call it a day, boys, I'm tired and I've had enough of wood work for the day," Harry suggested.

"Sure nuff, sounds good to me. I'm plum tuckered out. I think I'll sleep good tonight," Earl said, scratching his head.

The men headed to the house and around, coming onto the porch. Harry smiled at Marilyn who was holding Angela while Monroe ran up and down the hill, the dogs chasing him. He sat beside Marilyn and reached for the child and held her in his arms. He played patty cakes with her hands, causing her to giggle. Earl walked past and patted the baby on the head and then headed into the house.

Harry heard him laugh when the women said something. Clay came around the corner of the house and stepped up on the porch. He sat down in one of the rockers, and looked out over the valley. It was late afternoon, and the breeze had picked up.

"Getting a little airish," he said to no one in particular.

"Yeah, but I can't say I'm not enjoying it, I worked like a mule today," Harry said.

Boggy went into the house next and Harry heard him go upstairs. He suspected that the young man was going to wash up; he was very fastidious when it came to being clean. He suspected it was due to working in the coal mine. You might go in clean, but you came out coated in black dust.

Brian came back to the porch and laid down by Clay's feet panting heavily, his chest going up and down. Clay petted the dog's head.

"I'd say this is the most exercise Brian has ever had, I wish I had a fraction of the energy that Monroe has."

Harry laughed and set the wiggling Angela down, who tottered over to the dog and dug her fingers into his scruff. The dog was patient and closed his eyes, too tired to care.

"I can't imagine having that much energy, I could have cut down the whole forest with it," Harry said, using the handkerchief to wipe at his face.

"Monroe, you're too close to the barricade, come back up son," Marilyn called loudly, a clear warning in her voice.

She then jumped up, and Harry looked at her and then down the hill. A man had come through the bushes and had snatched up the boy, holding the wiggling child to his chest, a large knife held to the child's neck.

Marilyn grabbed Harry's arm in reflex and squeezed it, crying out in fear and anguish.

"I want food, I want lots of food. Send it down in a big poke, or I'll cut this young'un's throat. Now!" the filthy man screamed and jerked Monroe hard against him to stop the child squirming. Both dogs began barking, the hair standing rigid on their backs. Clay signaled Brian to quiet and the dog sat, though he whined in a low tone, his hair still erect. Charley was rushing in but not going close to the man and boy below.

"Get him what he wants," Harry said and disappeared into the house. He went upstairs into his room and shifted his rifle. He checked for a shell, then he zeroed in on the man below. His heart was hammering his chest and he felt the cold dread creep through his body. He could see that the man was filthy, in his late forties or older. He had a dirty gray beard and wild hair, his face gaunt beneath the filth and hair. His eyes were wild and he rocked back and forth with the child dangling from his arms.

Monroe was afraid, but didn't seem to be terrified. He waited and then saw Clay and Marilyn starting down the hill, carrying a pillowcase full of supplies.

"Just the woman," the man screamed, and he brought the knife up under Monroe's jaw. Harry hissed, anger moving through his veins. He could see blood running down the child's neck, it wasn't a lot, but the man had nicked the child's tender neck.

He watched Marilyn make her way down and she stumbled. He knew she was terrified for her son. She reached the man and held out a large pillowcase full of food. The man said something and she moved closer. He threw the boy aside, Charley running up to the boy and licking him. The man grabbed Marilyn and yanked her to him, his arm going around her waist, knife at her throat.

The breath left Harry as he saw the man dragging her backwards with him. If he got through the barricade, he could easily hurt Marilyn before they could get to her. His mouth tightened and he looked through the scope, lining up the shot. He hated that she was so close, but he couldn't let the man take her.

Taking a deep breath, he let it out, time slowing down in his brain and he caressed the trigger and made the shot. The stranger flew back and down, taking Marilyn with him, and for a terrifying moment, he was horrified he'd killed her, his heart dropping into his stomach and his mouth going dry as ash.

But then, he saw her struggling up. She was covered in blood, but as far as he could tell, she wasn't injured. She shoved off the dead man's arm, and staggered to her feet. She turned and looked down at the fallen man, wiping the blood from her face with her forearm. She then kicked the man hard three times, but he didn't move. She ran and picked Monroe up, holding the boy tight to her chest and started up the hill, looking back behind her.

Harry flew downstairs, his feet pounding the steps and then he ran out the door and off the porch, landing hard on the ground. He ran to Marilyn and caught her and Monroe in his arms and held them tight to his body.

"Christ, I thought I hit you Marilyn, I'm sorry, I had to make the shot, I couldn't let him take you past that barrier," he said, crushing Monroe between them. Monroe was squirming, but his small arms were wrapped around Harry's neck.

"You had no choice Harry, he wasn't going to let me go, he said so. Said I was his prize," Marilyn said in a shaky voice, her voice choking off.

Harry gave her a final hug, a kiss grazing her forehead and he pulled back, Monroe still attached to his neck, his face buried in Harry's chest. Harry hugged the boy, patting his narrow back and carried him up to the porch, as Boggy and Clay went down to take care of the body. When he passed Earl, the child reached out to him and Earl took the boy, holding him close to his chest. Earl's eyes were filled with unshed tears, his lips trembling. He looked at the child's neck and looked over to Katie who nodded and went into the house.

Willene was holding Angela to her, and went to Earl to look at Monroe's neck, which was still bleeding, but only a little. Katie came back out with her doctor's bag and opened it up. She pulled out sterile wipes and began to clean Monroe's neck, while Earl held him. Marilyn stood behind, rubbing the child's back. Monroe had stopped crying and held his arms around Earl's neck, a death grip.

"It looks superficial, no stitches will be needed. I will put ointment on it and we'll leave it to air dry. He's had his tetanus shot?" Katie said, looking up at Marilyn who nodded.

"That was too close, we need to put a line across those apple trees, so Monroe knows not to go beyond that point. Maybe put little flags on them, like a reminder," Willene suggested.

"I think that is a wonderful idea, maybe also twenty feet before each tree line," Marilyn added, her voice still shaking. She sat down beside Earl on the swing, he was holding Monroe in his lap, rocking him, rubbing the child's back.

"I thought that stranger was gonna hurt this baby," Earl said finally, finding his voice, which trembled.

"I think he would have, and worse had he not gotten the food and me," Marilyn said, her hands shaking as she smoothed back her hair.

"I wonder why the dogs didn't pick him up?" Katie asked.

"He may have been down there for quite a while. And he was filthy as hell, they may not have recognized the smell. Or he could have covered his scent," Harry guessed.

"He smelled horrible, like rotted meat and feces," Marilyn said and shuddered.

"Maybe Clay can train Charley to patrol and guard," Willene suggested, setting Angela down on the porch to play. She toddled over to Charley who was panting on the porch. Everyone looked down at the dog.

"My god, that was too close," Katie said, her face pale.

"I'm damn glad you're a good shot brother," Willene said and patted Harry on his shoulders. His shoulders felt tight and he shifted them a bit to ease the tension. It had been close, too close and he stopped himself from thinking and imagining the worst.

A while later, Clay and Boggy were coming up the hill, both sweating profusely.

"We found a deep trench about thirty feet into the tree line. There was a bunch of apple cores there, and some green beans. I think he's been here a while, watching us," Clay said, when they reached the porch.

"Jesus." Marilyn breathed. Everyone looked at each other, and then the dogs.

"There's no telling when he came, maybe in the night, but looks like he's been there at least a week. He defecated right by the trench, it really stinks down there. We took the body about a mile down the road and took it into the woods."

"I don't think we should burry that trash, just throw him out," Boggy said, anger lacing his voice, his mouth drawn down and his dark brows knotted. Harry guessed he was also thinking about the two men he'd killed.

"I agree, but I think we should load him up later and drive him farther away. I don't want to smell that stench. My god, right in our own front yard, watching us," Harry said, shaking his head.

"I think that is an unusual occurrence, I think he just stank so badly, not like human or animal, the dogs didn't know what it was and he'd had been here so long, they became nose deaf maybe," Clay suggested.

"I sure do hope so, I'd hate ta think there'd be more of that kind around," Earl said. He set Monroe down, who went over to sit by Brian, the child accepting licks to his face from the dog.

"I hate to say it, but that may be exactly what we get. People are starving, especially if they'd not put anything aside, or hoped the government would come to help," Harry said.

"I'm afraid to say it, but you're probably right Harry. There is no telling where he came from, maybe Lexington, maybe from farther out," Katie said, shaking her head.

Marilyn came back out in clean clothing. She'd washed her face and upper body. She paused, looking at her son. Harry was once more reminded how close he came to shooting her. It shook him to his core. He'd never wanted to experience that fear and uncertainty again.

"I'd say we might want to put some kind of alarm system around the garden, looks like he was in it. Maybe we can tie Charley out there at night, instead of him sleeping in the house," Willene said, eyeing the dog.

"Yeah, make him earn his dinner," Harry said and laughed, though it wasn't much of a laugh; he felt sick to his stomach at the near tragedy.

"Good idea, because all someone has to do is make sure we're on the other side of the property, then sneak into the garden and steal from us," Marilyn said sitting down beside Harry. He reached over and squeezed her and she smiled up at him reassuringly. Monroe came back over to her and she hugged and kissed him. He then returned back to the dog.

"I think we need ta build a couple more foxholes," Boggy suggested.

"Tomorrow, I'll dig two more, and use the door from them cars," Earl volunteered.

"I'll go finish dinner, we're having chicken stew. I've also made cornbread, though I'll warn you now, it is a little burnt around the edges," Willene said.

"I like burnt. I'll also pluck the turkey after dinner," Clay said and grinned.

"I think I will draw up plans for a dog house for Charley, I'll make it tomorrow and put it by the garden. That will be his new duty station until all the crops are in," Harry said, his eyes narrowing in on the dog.

It was dark, the clouds obliterating the moon and stars. Monroe was tucked up in his bed, sound asleep and seemed to have shaken off the fear of earlier that afternoon. Harry sat smoking his pipe, he was in the swing with Marilyn. Boggy was on patrol, and had started going into the tree line, deeper with the NVGs.

He and Clay had gone to retrieve the dead man earlier. They'd driven five miles and found a suitable spot to dump the body. It was rank and Harry was loathe to touch him. Willene had given him and Clay rubber gloves to handle the dead man. He was glad. Thinking about it made him shiver.

Katie and Clay were talking quietly in the glider and Earl was sitting on the edge of the porch beside Willene. They were talking about high school and Harry heard them laugh a few times. He grinned when he saw Earl smile.

Just before dinner, he'd presented Earl with his grandfather's false teeth. With all the hell that had broken loose, he'd almost forgotten. He and Willene had modified them, taking a small fine blade saw and cutting down on the farther back portion, taking it off. Earl still had most of his molars. He was missing all of his front teeth, which had been kicked out by his ex-friend, Hobo. He'd also lost a few in a mining accident years ago, but Hobo had kindly finished the job.

Once his gums healed, Willene had informed Harry, she'd wanted to modify their grandfather's dentures.

"I'm not sure it will even work, but if we can cut the back portion off and file and buff it down until it is smooth, I think Earl might be able to wear them. They had roughly the same jaw structure and size," she said.

Once they'd reduced the size, Harry had taken sand paper and had sanded the rough edges smooth, then had buffed them, both the lower and upper dentures. They had boiled water and put them in it, until they were slightly flexible. He had filed and buffed again until they were completely smooth.

Just before dinner, Harry pulled Earl aside and showed him the dentures. Earl stared at them, then looked at Harry, puzzled.

"Willene thinks you'd be able to wear these. We've cut them down and I think they may fit you. If they are too tight or too loose, we can boil them and maybe do more adjustments. They've been sterilized too," Harry said, shrugging and turning red. He hadn't been sure he'd maybe stepped over the line.

"Well, sure, I'll give it a try," he said and took the dentures and fitting first the lower set. He moved his jaw around experimentally. His eye brows going up.

173

"I shink thatsh fish ood," he said and grinned with the bottom teeth showing.

He fit the uppers in and shifted them back and forth a bit, then chomped a few times and grinned with a perfect set of teeth; he ran to the bathroom and looked in the mirror. He turned and grinned at Harry, tears in his eyes.

"I fergit whash itsh like ta has teesh," Earl said and wiped his eyes.

"There is plenty of Fixodent in the cupboard in the main bathroom. Willene said not to wear them too long or you'll get blisters, but let your gums toughen up over time," Harry said, his throat thick with emotion. It never occurred to him to give him his grandfather's dentures, yet Willene had thought of it when Earl had come back to the house with all his front teeth missing.

"I shay, I a hanshum devil." Earl grinned once more at himself in the mirror, and both men headed down to dinner. Everyone stopped and looked and made a big fuss of how wonderful he looked.

"You just got handsomer," Boggy said and grinned good-naturedly, causing everyone to laugh and slap Earl on the back.

Earl seemed to be more animated now, and Willene was laughing and nodding. He saw Willene bump the man with her shoulder. Her shoulders going up and down as they laughed.

He was about to ask Marilyn about Monroe, when everyone paused in talking. In the distance, they saw a glow and knew headlights were heading their way. The glow moved and then came around a curve. They waited to see if it would pass. It got up to the barricade and began to slow down but went past. It stopped some ways up the road and they heard the engine stop.

"Maybe that's Alan," Marilyn whispered.

"I hope so, I've been wanting to know what is going on," Harry said.

Everyone waited silently and they saw a wavering light coming back up the road. Someone was walking back. Then they saw the light flicker wildly through the barricade and then someone popped through.

The person pointed the flashlight at his face; it was Alan and he had his eyes squinted shut and waved. Then he made his way up the hill. Harry laughed and got up, exhaling. He'd held his breath until he knew it was the boy. He heard Clay exhale and smiled. He wasn't the only one.

Alan climbed up the steps to the porch and Willene walked over and gave him a hug. "Are you hungry honey?" she asked.

"I could eat," he said grinning and she laughed and went into the darkened house.

Katie gave him a hug as well and he grinned broadly and then Marilyn gave him a hug. Harry told him to take a seat.

"How have you been Alan, we've been wondering and worried for you. How is your grandfather?" Harry asked.

"We're good, and Pop Pop is causing lots a trouble," Alan said and laughed. Harry smiled, it was good to hear the boy laugh, especially after the last encounter.

"What's your grandfather up to?" Harry asked, grinning.

"He and his old buddies, most is ex-military, been shootin them KKK boys. Pickin them off. That mayor, or president is madder'n a wet hen about it." He sniggered and everyone joined in.

Willene came out with a bowl of chicken stew and a chunk of cornbread and some sweet tea. Marilyn got up and got a folding TV tray and set in front of the boy. Willene set the food and drink on it and then sat back down. Everyone waited for a few minutes until Alan had taken a few bites and then came up for air. Harry grinned in the dark, teens were perpetually hungry, especially now.

"That's great news. Did he ever get in touch with my cousin Boney?" Clay asked.

"Oh sure, and they're good friends. Even though Boney's Marine and Pop Pop is Army, but they pick on Mr. Sherman Collins on count he's Navy," Alan said with a titter.

"Hey now, I was Navy," Clay said.

Harry laughed hard, "swabby," he said good naturedly.

Everyone laughed and then they heard Boggy coming in and he came up onto the porch. He went to Alan and shook the young man's hand.

"How's ya been?" Boggy asked.

"I've been good, n you?" Alan asked.

"I guess I'll do," Boggy said grinning, and went to sit on the edge of the porch by Willene and Earl.

"I came ta let ya know that they're getting them young'uns out of the coal mine. They're smugglin them out and taking them to the Friedhof's farm. Mrs. Mary Deets, she be pregnant, they got her out. They're afraid she's gonna lose that young'un," he said, taking another bite of stew and cornbread, then washed them down with the sweet tea.

"Oh, thank god, at least the children will be out of there," Willene said.

"Mary Deets was in the coal mine? Where's her husband, Howard?" Clay asked suddenly, sitting forward.

"I'm sorry ta say Clay, that sheriff done killed Officer Deets on that first day. Then they throwed his wife in the mine," Alan said, sadness in his voice.

Clay made a choking noise and Katie placed her arm around his shoulders.

"Howard was a good man, a real good man. Are Mary and the baby, okay?" Clay asked, choked with emotion.

"She is now, Jutta done shaked the hell out of them boys, said she'd gut them if they'd told Mary was there. They ain't said a peep," Alan said with satisfaction.

"I heard that Jutta done broke some woman's legs for look'n at Gerhard," Earl said.

"I'm so sorry Clay, we'd not gotten word of who was killed and who was put in the mine," Willene said, sorrow heavy in her voice.

"I'm sorry as well Clay. I am glad to hear his wife is safe now. That is some good news about the unrest with Audrey's men. It means that some of the men aren't hard line behind Audrey and Yates," Harry said.

Clay smiled and nodded; his face drawn with sorrow. He got up and left the porch. Harry thought perhaps he needed some time alone to grieve for his friend. He noticed Katie watching him, concern on her face.

"I think that folks are realizing mayor ain't gonna share no vittles. I think they're getting mad. I heard Mrs. Jutta knocked the woman's teeth out an pulled all her hair out," Alan said. He had a smile on his homely face, his big ears sticking out like standards.

"That's the best news I've heard in a while. I've heard Jutta broke both the woman's arms," Marilyn said.

"Now, if your grandfather and his friends can stir up the hornets' nest a little more, I think we might well have a chance at turning the tide. And no, Jutta ran over a woman for smacking her kid, she only clipped the woman I believe. They didn't arrest her though," Harry said.

Everyone breathed a collective "ooohhhhhh." Harry was sure the whole town had some explanation for what happened with Jutta. He was sure they were all wrong.

"Old Andy had a heart attack, I think. I was behind him when his truck hit a tree. I checked and he was stone dead. Had boxes of food in the back of the truck. I took it, and I'm giving it ta folks that need it," Alan said with a smirk.

Earl shook his head. "Lil by little, that mayor gonna learn a hard lesson."

"The mayor and the sheriff need a swift kick in the ass," Willene said.

"They need a bullet, right between their eyes," Clay said stonily. He'd come back around to the porch, and stood in the dark. The group grew quiet and Alan's eating was the only sound in the night.

CHAPTER EIGHT

Bella May was in her kitchen; peeling potatoes for some nice stew. She softly hummed under her breath. She had already cleaned some carrots from the garden. She was pleased that her garden was doing great, it certainly made for tastier meals. She'd also canned some of the potatoes, beans, tomatoes and carrots as well as some of the meat. She had zucchini that was out back; she was dehydrating them into chips. She'd set up an old window, then she had angled it so it would receive the most sunlight during the day.

She set the zucchini slices on a screen she'd scrubbed clean. She was also trying to do the green beans, tomato slices as well. She had to think of long-term food now. Thank goodness she had Hobo, what a godsend. She was wiping her hands on her apron when she heard a loud knock at her door. She looked over to the basement door, it was shut. Once more she thanked her forethought years ago. The basement was soundproof, and again, she'd badgered her husband to get it done. She laughed and shook her head. If it wasn't for her pushing so hard for what she wanted, she'd have shoddy work.

Going to the front door, she opened it, and found a short police officer standing before her.

Her heart slammed into her chest. She stared at him blankly and he stepped in rudely, pushing her aside roughly. The man walked around, looking at the fallen hutch. Then he walked into the kitchen.

"You got food here. You got more of this?" he said brusquely.

"What? What do you mean officer? Are you hungry?" she asked, her green eyes large and innocent looking. She didn't let the rage show from his arrogance and obnoxious behavior.

"I'm askin if you got more food? I'm here ta confiscate it on orders from the president. And to also ask if you'd heard about someone shooting our people," he said, his mouth turned down, his brown eyes narrowing. She thought they looked like shit brown.

"Why's the president want my food, don't they got food in Washington?" she asked, confused.

"Stupid woman, President Audrey," he said, his anger and impatience beginning to show.

"I thought he was the mayor," she said simply.

"Shut the hell up woman and show me where you keep your food," he said, pointing a finger at her.

"Of course, Officer Smalls," she said, looking at his name tag. She pointed to the basement door. "Most of my food is in the basement, it is cooler down there. You can take as much as you need officer," she said kindly.

He nodded shortly and shoved past her, causing her to stumble back and went to the door of the basement and opened it. Smalls turned his head to say something, when Bella May shoved the man between his shoulders as hard as she could. Smalls was launched into the air and fell like a stone, bouncing on the stairs, screaming and then went silent. Bella May smiled broadly.

"Make yourself comfortable peckerwood, I'll be right back," she said and laughed, and turned closing the door.

She went to the front door and looked out. There was a lone horse tethered to her mail box. She walked to the horse and untied the reins and smacked the horse on the rump and sent it running away. She smiled, watching it go and turned, humming, and went back into her house.

She got her solar lantern and made her way downstairs. She saw the officer laying on the floor, one foot still on the step. He was bleeding from his head. She went back upstairs and got one of her heavy oak chairs. Then she went to the garage and got several lengths of chain. She went back and forth until she had all she needed.

She pulled the heavy chair over and used her battery-operated drill with a tipped hole cutter. Then she changed and used her jigsaw to cut a larger hole. She pushed hard; she could tell the battery was beginning to lose its strength. It would be a hard task once the jigsaw lost power. She sighed in relief when a good size chunk fell. She'd have to do another chair later, before the battery died completely. Just in case she had another visitor. She sniggered to herself.

She placed a five-gallon bucket below and then went to the unconscious man. She looked up at Hobo, who had been quiet all along.

"You have a friend, some company," she said and grinned, then she laughed.

Hobo said nothing, he looked at his right side, one arm missing, up to his shoulder. He looked to the left, only his upper arm was still there. He looked over at the smaller man. A smile quaked on his thin lips. Bella May laughed and began to undress the man. She then tied ropes under him and used the pulley and crank to haul him up into the chair. He slipped and slid but she managed to get him into place. She then began to chain him to the steel support beam.

She tugged and grunted, pulling it tight. She secured his arms next; she brought out her handy duct tape. She pulled a bit and taped his upper arms and then forearms and then chained those as well. Next, she chained his thighs, legs and ankles. She also taped his penis, pointing down into the bucket. Satisfied he was well secured; she turned and went back upstairs. She heard Hobo laughing and shook her head.

She came back down with her pot of vegetables; she looked over at Hobo who'd stopped laughing at her descent into the basement. She brought over the wooden stool and placed it under Smalls' hand. Then she put the pot beneath his hand. She then got her bundle and opened it on the table. She walked to the unconscious officer and wiped and cleaned his hand. She then took the scalpel from her apron, this one had butterflies on it, and began to cut around the wrist. Blood began to pour into the pot below and she placed small vascular clamps on the radial artery and ulnar artery. Then she retrieved the small saw and began to saw the hand off.

She heard Hobo begin to gag and she stopped and looked over at him.

"What's a matter?" she asked, smiling at him. He said nothing.

"At least it won't be you for a while. Relax and enjoy. He is an asshole, just like you," she said and she turned back and finished sawing the hand off. She took the hand and cut off the fingernails, and then tossed the whole hand into the pot. She then pulled up the wooden stool and sat on it. There was a bowl in her lap to catch the blood. She cleaned the wound and began to sew it up quickly. She put ointment on it and got up. She went back to the small stove and looked in the pot. She stirred the contents and then added some spices and then put a lid on the pot and turned the flame down.

She let out a satisfied breath and went to her lounger and picked up her knitting. She looked up at Hobo, who was looking at the unconscious man. She shook her head and started knitting, waiting for her dinner and her new guest to wake up.

□

Wilber and Boney had separated from the larger group. They would go on to their targets tonight. Each man had chosen a target, the Edison twins were very happy about that. They'd each chosen a man. The old men were like boys, giggling and making jokes, shoving each other. They sniggered and acted silly; they were all in high spirits.

Wilber knew that they all felt young again and useful. He'd not told Alan what was going on tonight, he didn't want his grandson to worry. He'd left out just after midnight, his grandson passed out in his room. He'd looked in on the boy before he'd left and smiled softly. The kid was dead to the world. He envied that kind of sleep. Nowadays, he was up and down all night. Aches and pains kept him awake most nights.

Tonight however, he felt no pain, his heart racing in anticipation. They all knew what was at stake and knew also that they may well be killed, but to go out in a blaze of glory, instead of rotting in a chair. They had all been in battle, *well except for Collins, he was a Squiddly Diddly and didn't do diddly and they didn't count* he sniggered to himself. Well, Collins was in Vietnam, but he wasn't really shot at. Well, not much.

Wilber lifted his hand in farewell, he had chosen the bastard who'd shot that kid who'd flipped off the mayor. He'd found out where the peckerwood lived and was heading there now. He lived in an apartment, so it would be a tricky kill. In his pocket was a brick, he carried it with him. He'd thought about it a lot and he figured if he threw the brick through the peckerwood's window, it was sure to lure him out. He'd have to get his aim right the first time. He'd not get a second chance.

He didn't need anyone seeing him after the initial shot. That would give the game away. His face had ash and bootblack, so his features were hidden, but his body was old and he didn't move as fast. He didn't need a bullet in the back from a sympathizing pecker-head friend. The shit-heel was a cockroach, and where there was one cockroach, there were more. He hoped he'd have a good vantage point at the kill site.

Alan had gone to visit his friends the previous day; he was glad the boy had a safe place to go. If anything were to happen, he'd left a letter for the boy, telling him to go and live with his friends. He also wrote in the letter, *don't grieve, I will die with valor and honor, doing what needs to be done.* Wilber wasn't an overly sentimental man, but he loved his grandson dearly.

Wilber inhaled deeply and pulled a cigarette out and lit it. He inhaled a long drag of the cigarette; he held it in his lungs and then let it out slowly. He loved the damn things, didn't give a shit that they'd kill him eventually, something in this life would. No one got out alive in this world, no matter how rich or how poor, how smart or stupid. He hoped he could meet death bravely. He'd hate to think after all these years, that he was a coward.

He was getting close to the complex and dropped the butt and crushed it. He listened intently, but heard nothing. It was quiet, but for the insects and the rustling of the branches above in the trees. There was a breeze blowing and he could feel the chill of it. Autumn wasn't far off and then the snow would come. He shivered thinking about the coming winter.

He found an abandoned car that was directly across from the apartment door. He calculated the distance between the car and the window, about twenty feet. He thought he could run it pretty quick for a short distance. He first went to the abandoned car and set his rifle on the roof of the car. He flipped up the night optics on the weapon and zeroed in on the door.

He looked up and around then back to the scope. It felt comfortable. He laid the rifle on its side on the roof of the car and went around. He stood roughly ten feet from the apartment. Pausing, he looked around once more, into the windows and around him. He heard and saw nothing. He pulled back his arm, hurled the brick with all his might. As it left his hand, he'd already turned and Wilber bent at the waist and ran like hell to the car.

There was a satisfying crash of the window shattering. He picked up his gun and aimed it for the door. He waited, double checking his aim. It was maybe ten seconds later that a squat fat man ran out in his underwear. His hair was wild from sleep and he jerked, looking around. He had a weapon and he was looking around wildly. Wilber took careful aim, this had to count. He pulled the trigger and the man jerked back like a puppet with his strings cut and went down in a crumpled bloody heap.

Wilber stood and turned, retreating back the way he came, walking quickly, but not running. He didn't need to trip in the dark. Keeping to the shadows, he looked back over his shoulder. He saw people looking through their windows, but no one came out, fear keeping them caged in their homes. All the better, no collateral damage and no witnesses.

Wilber felt elated, he'd avenged that boy, he'd gotten another target. This was great, if they could go out every once and a while and hunt, nothing too organized, they could make a dent in these peckerwoods. He then heard some shouts, and knew someone was aware of the kill. He picked up his pace and headed for the nearest tree line. He needed to get out of the area fast.

He knew the area well, he'd lived and worked in Beattyville all his life. He went through another apartment complex, slipping easily out of range and sight of the other apartment complex. In the distance, he heard an engine. But it was far away. He shook his head grinning. It took nearly twenty minutes, but he made it back to the truck. He got in and sat back and sighed happily. He hoped the other boys were getting their targets.

☐

Vern began to rouse; he felt a throbbing pain in his head and his hand. He couldn't remember what had happened. He could see light, but it was all blurry, like there was petroleum jelly over his eyes. He blinked rapidly and tried to shake his head, but that hurt like hell and made him groan.

"Hey Vern, how ya doin?" a voice sniggered. It sounded familiar, but he couldn't place it.

190

"Who's there?" he asked, his mouth dry as cotton and he swallowed hard. He gritted his teeth in pain, it was as though he were trying to swallow a stickaburr.

"It's me, Hobo. You is fucked," Hobo said and started laughing hard.

"Now Hobo, don't be naughty," a woman's voice said.

"Who is there? Who are you?" he asked the woman.

"That be Karma," Hobo said nodding toward her, and the woman laughed.

"What?" Vern said confused. He kept blinking, furiously and then he noticed that he couldn't move. He tried to wiggle, but nothing moved. His ass hurt, and it felt numb. Slowly, his vision began to clear. In front of him was a naked man with an arm missing and part of another arm, cut off at the elbow. His brain was trying to figure that out, when he recognized Hobo. He'd arrested the shit three times, and three times he'd vomited on him.

"Hobo? What the hell you doing neked?" Vern asked, and thought maybe he was hallucinating. Or perhaps he was having a nightmare, though he'd never had anything so real like this, nor as bizarre as this.

Hobo was chained to a steel post and sitting in a chair. Then his eyes shifted and he saw an old woman in a lounger, knitting. It was so inexplicable to him, he laughed. He knew he must be having a dream. He shivered, his body feeling cold, but he was dreaming. He couldn't remember if in his other dreams he felt cold or not.

"What's so funny?" Hobo asked.

"I'm dreaming," Vern said, smiling.

"No, you ain't boy, you is fucked, just like me," Hobo said, a wide crazed grin on his face.

Vern looked over to the old woman who nodded, a beaming smile on her withered face. He now remembered she'd been the woman he'd been talking to about food. He didn't remember what had happened, but there she was, knitting. It occurred to him then to look down and he was shocked and embarrassed that he was naked.

Then he realized he had chains around his body, his arms and legs and he was duct taped as well and then he saw his hand and screamed, long and loud. Hobo began to laugh hysterically, spittle dripping from his open mouth, his meth teeth crusted with scum.

Vern stared at him in horror, his eyes wide as the screams kept coming out. He saw that Hobo was laughing and he glimpsed madness in those laughing eyes. He couldn't stop screaming, when he saw the stump where his hand should have been. And his body felt colder, dread and terror bumping up on his skin as it rippled across his body like an avalanche.

"That's enough Hobo, leave him be," the woman said. She got up and walked over to Vern, and grabbed his chin and drew his attention to her. She squeezed painfully on his jaw and he stopped screaming.

"Vern, I'm Bella May. You are in my basement," she said calmly.

"Why, why am I here in your basement?" Vern asked, his brown eyes frantic, desperately trying to grasp some kind of sanity in this nightmare.

"You don't wanna know that," Hobo giggled, in a sing song voice.

"Hobo. You need to hush," Bella May warned, her voice still soft. Hobo didn't say another word.

"Vern, you came into my home, you didn't even ask to come in, you just barged into my home. You demanded food and shoved me around. You didn't even ask and you called me stupid. Did you know that *stupid* is my trigger word? My father used to call me stupid. And it has always made me want to kill," she said, her green eyes boring savagely into his brown eyes, that were large and frightened.

"I'm sorry, I'm sorry," he said, his voice shaking.

"I know you are Vern, but it is too late for sorry. You see, Hobo over there, he came uninvited into my home as well. He'll never leave, and neither will you. You're both my protein," she said.

"Pr.. protein?" Vern stammered, spit hitting his chin.

"Yes, Vern, you see, I need an inordinate amount of meat. I'm too old to go hunting anymore, so like a spider, I have to wait for something to come into my web. You Vern Smalls, barged into my web."

Vern began to cry and looked at his stump and then her and then Hobo.

"Please no, please no. I'll leave, I won't come back and I won't tell anyone. Please, let me go. I'll even bring you meat, I swear, I'll hunt for you," Vern begged, his lips pulled back in a grimace of utter fear.

"Now that's an idea. But no, I know what kind of man you are, just like my dear old dad. Well, dear old dad didn't make it out of here on his last visit," she said smiling and that smile sent a shiver down to his internal vestigial tail. He could feel it tingle there and felt his scrotum pull up into his body from the primordial fear.

"Vern, I can see you're much brighter than yonder there," she said, nodding her head toward Hobo, who was biting his lower lip.

"Vern, you and Hobo are my protein, I'll be eating you. As you can see, Hobo has been here a while. Now that you're here, he gets a break. Sorry, that's just how it goes. Guess you shouldn't have knocked on my door and barged in," she said, a soft smile on her mouth.

Vern looked at her mouth and then his hand. He wanted to weep; he couldn't get out of this. He didn't believe it, but he couldn't get out of this. He tried to move his body, but he was tightly secure. He looked at his stump where his missing hand used to be. He saw the redness and the neat stitching. It glistened obscenely with ointment.

"Will you at least numb it up?" he asked, his voice cracking, he could feel hot tears cascading down his face.

"Sorry Vern, but I don't have anything to numb it, but don't worry, when I start to saw, you'll pass out." She grinned and went back to her recliner to pick up her knitting. Stunned, he stared at her and then he looked over at Hobo, who was rocking slightly, grinning. He could do nothing except let the tears fall and stare.

☐

Danny Yates sat at his desk, and looked up when Grady came running in.

"Sheriff, we got trouble, there's a group of strangers that's come into town. They got weapons, and they ain't given over."

195

Yates blew out a breath, he'd been afraid of this. Lexington was an hour or better away by car, but people could still make their way here. They couldn't afford to have strangers just show up; they didn't have the resources to absorb them.

"Go and get your people, have 'em bring their weapons, we got to kill 'em. Can't let them leave or they'll be back," he said resigned. He grabbed his service revolver and checked it. He then opened a drawer and pulled out a Glock, which had been confiscated. He checked the magazine and put it back. Both weapons smelled of gun oil. He'd cleaned them the previous week. He'd not had to use them since he'd shot Deets.

Grady disappeared and Yates walked out of his office and made his way to the street. He had a cigar clamped tight in his teeth. He saw several of the townspeople and nodded to them, but they turned and ran in the opposite direction. He laughed softly and shrugged. It was then he realized he was carrying the Glock. He walked up the street, looking down side streets as he went. He didn't know where the newcomers were, but he was sure they were close by.

Grady came running back, with five men, each carried a weapon. One toted an AR-15. Another a shotgun, the other three possessed hunting rifles. The men walked silently, Yates and Grady in the lead.

"Make damn sure you don't shoot me or Grady for Christ's sake. Check for crossfire," he said over his shoulder to the other men.

Up the street, they heard yelling and then a gunshot sounded and Yates picked up his speed. At the Quick-Mart, one of his people lay dead on the sidewalk; the group of eight people were walking into the store. Taking aim, Yates began to fire with the Glock, dropping three people before they could turn around.

Yates grinned; he had not won the annual regional championship target shoot for nothing. He smiled, the cigar still clamped, but to the side of his mouth. He chewed on the end of it and switched it to the other side of his mouth. He scanned the area.

The man with the AR-15 began to pepper the people who tried to scatter, and Grady and the other men picked them off; they stood behind abandon vehicles. From inside the store, there was shooting and Yates took cover behind an abandoned truck.

"Get around back and pick them off. If they come out this way, we'll get them," he ordered Grady and two men with the hunting rifles.

Grady and the two men ran across the street, fifty feet up and to the right of the store. Yates watched as they kept low and used the vehicles as barriers. Yates waited patiently, and then he heard shots from the back of the store. Then a man came running out, a big man and he took careful aim and shot him, dropping him.

He stood and sauntered over and looked down. The man was wheezing and bubbling blood from his nose and mouth. Yates smiled and looked down into the man's eyes. He aimed the Glock and fired. He glanced up as Grady rushed through the door and smiled.

"Have your people clean this shit up. Good work," he said, looking around at the dead men and women. He didn't recognize any of them, they weren't from town.

"Once this is cleared, take the bodies to the main roads leading into town. Set up road blocks, and put these bodies there as a warning. Make up a sign, *Outsiders Not Welcome* and leave the bodies to rot. I want two men at each road block."

"But Preside..." Grady was saying, before Yates cut him off.

"I don't give two rat fucks what he wants, I said do it. I'll worry about the mayor."

Yates turned and looked down and spat on the big man's face and turned and walked back to his office. He needed a drink. He knew that there would be more outsiders coming their way. This was simply the first. He was surprised that it had taken as long as it had. He suspected these idiots had eaten their way to Beattyville.

He was getting tired of having the tug of war with the men. Audrey wanted to be surrounded, but with all the recent deaths of their men, they were becoming dangerously thin. They needed to find who was picking them off. It could be anyone with a rifle. There were many hunters in this community. Heck, most men lived for hunting season. He'd have to get with Audrey and pry some of his men lose to go on patrols.

He shook his head at the thought of Audrey, he was useless, worse than useless. The bastard was eating up supplies and assets. Something had to give. He couldn't do all this on his own. Where the hell was Vern? The man had gone missing a couple of days ago. He wondered if the man had deserted camp. He'd not be surprised. Confidence was low.

☐

David and the crew stepped off the bus, they'd brought the last two children, Steven and Boyd, Gideon, Julia's boys. The boys walked into the house to be cleaned and fed. The guards had finally been drawn to their side. It seemed that one of the guards, Richard Bibs's mother, was a Patterson, and third cousin to Clay Patterson, who was sixth cousin to Boney Patterson.

On their last visit, Richard grew a conscience; when he also found out that Mary was related by marriage by a fourth cousin, he'd wept at her feet, pleading for forgiveness.   Both he and Bill Hawkins had gone over to the right side. Bill had let it slip that his wife was also pregnant, and he'd gone to the mayor for more food and had been denied. When Jutta had kindly given him food for his pregnant wife, Bill wept. He'd asked Mary for forgiveness, as had Richard.

When Mary asked them why they hated blacks so much, neither men knew why. David shook his head, and wondered at the parents of so many people.

"It's just always been that way since I was a young'un," Bill said, turning bright red. "I always heard my ma and pa, and granny and grandpa too. They always said bad things. I just learned it."

Richard shook his head sadly. "My parents was always ashamed of our relatives, and said we can't tell nobody nothing. If I had said something, they'd whooped the tar outta me. I'd didn't know any better," he said, his face filled with shame.

"You know, now don't you? Do you see how hurtful and brutal it is? Richard, we're all family, and we are all we have got now that the world has ended," Mary said. Richard began to cry once more, sorrowful sobs. Jutta turned her head and hid a smile, but Mary and David caught it. He hid his own smile, as did Mary.

They said their parents had taught them blacks were bad people, lazy and dirty. They'd trusted their parent's beliefs and had never called them into question, until now. Until they saw what the harsh bigotry had wrought, something ugly, violent and deadly. David thought Mary had been very kind; she had forgiven the men. David was stymied about all the hurtfulness and the hating. It did no one any good.

Miles Whitman was the driver, he never said a word, but his eyes told everything. He was ashamed as well and when the last two boys got off the bus, he laid his head on the steering wheel and wept. The two boys had been horribly thin, on the edge of cadaverous. Most teen boys notoriously had high metabolisms; their bodies had greedily eaten every calorie but it hadn't been enough.

David watched the guards look at the boys, their lips trembling. The boys were wretched looking and that broke David's heart. He looked down at his own body, which had been robust, but was now incredibly thin. The food here helped a great deal, but they were all still working hard in the fields, burning the calories fast. One step forward, two steps back.

It seemed like Sheriff Yates and Mayor Audrey were driving this train, with the help of a few key people in power. He and Mary talked about it, and David thought that if they could topple Yates and Audrey, and their higher up

KKK brethren, and just maybe turn the others, then maybe they could end this travesty. He saw Gerhard and walked over, shaking the man's hand.

"That's the last of the children. Thank you for taking them. I know it is a lot of mouths to feed," David said.

"They're welcome here, Jutta wouldn't have it any other way. That mayor said he'd want most of the crops, but he ain't getting much. We're making sure it gets put away, somewhere safe," Gerhard said smiling.

"You don't think he'll notice?" David asked, concern that Gerhard might have trouble look his way.

"If his lard ass would leave town, I guess he'd know. But we both know he ain't leave'en," Gerhard said laughing and David joined him.

Jutta came back out with Mary. It looked to David that she'd started putting on weight, he'd noticed this visit. He was always glad to see her. She walked up to him and gave him a hug. He grinned down at her.

"You're looking a lot better Mary, you have color to your cheeks. You were looking kinda gray. How is the baby?" he asked, smiling down at her.

"Good, moving a lot, and thanks to Jutta, I'm sure I've gained at least five pounds. She stuffs me full every chance she gets," Mary said and laughed, her small hand going to her hair.

"I'm glad. I'm glad you're feeling better too. I'm going to wash up and get breakfast and head out to the fields," he said.

"What are y'all doing today?" she asked.

"We'll be finishing up the taters, then head over to the corn fields. Most of the corn will be left for silage; there are some fields with sweet corn as well. We'll get those picked; Jutta wants to start canning that. She also plans to dry some out, for grinding," he said, hands in his pockets. It was hard to be around Mary and not want to hold on to her. He'd realized that he'd fallen in love with her. This wasn't good, because she was grieving for Howard. Howard was a good man and he'd not do anything to shame himself or the man's memory.

He lifted his hand in farewell and went to the barn. He hoped that one day, when a good amount of time had passed, that perhaps he'd pursue a relationship with her. For now, he was satisfied with being her friend. She had enough on her shoulders right now; she didn't need the complication of a love-sick man.

Clay and Katie walked along the perimeter of the property, going into the tree line about thirty feet. Both were quiet, each in their own thoughts. Katie had the watch, but Clay had accompanied her. They had begun to get close again. Their romantic relationship picking up where they'd left off. He cared about her deeply and always had. They'd broken up because both were so busy in their careers that they had little time for dating.

Now, they had all the time in the world. He took her small hand and smiled down at her. She looked up and returned the smile and squeezed his hand. He could hear Brian ahead, rustling through the undergrowth and he grinned.

"I think Brian gets more out of these patrols than we do," he said.

"Agreed. I think he has more fun anyway."

Both stopped for a moment, listening intently. They scanned the surrounding woods, hearing and seeing nothing, they resumed their walk. Their footfalls were quiet except for the occasional snapping of a twig. Clay felt the cool wind coming from the south. It had the hint of smoke and something else. He wasn't sure.

"I hope that is a cook fire and not a forest fire," he said, picking up his pace.

"It isn't strong, perhaps it just picked up from the wind."

"Might be, let's head farther south, work our way over and down," he said, leading her.

They walked farther away from the house and deeper into the woods. They continued walking for nearly twenty minutes but saw nothing. The wind had shifted and the smell of smoke was gone.

"Maybe it was a cook fire." He sighed and stood for a moment looking around. "Let's head back, I don't think it is anything close."

They turned back the way they'd come, and saw Brian ahead of them. It looked like he'd cornered something and Clay picked up his step. Katie keeping up.

"What do you think he's found?" she asked.

"Don't know."

They came up and Katie gasped in horror. Beneath branches and leaves was a child. So thin, its bones etched out clear beneath the pale dirty skin. Clay took a knee and gently placed two fingers under the child's thin neck.

"He's still warm, and I think I feel a pulse. Can you check him?" Clay asked, looking up helplessly at Katie. She quickly knelt down beside him and they rolled the child over. The boy, who looked to be about five, moaned softly.

"Let's get him to the house quickly," she said and Clay picked the boy up gently. He weighed nothing, he was skin and bones. Clay ran ahead, hoping Katie could keep up. He curled his body around the boy, protecting him from branches that scraped at Clay as he passed through the trees.

It took an agonizing ten minutes to reach the edge of the tree line and he looked behind, Katie was about ten yards behind. He paused a moment to wait for her to catch up. His heart was beating heavily in his chest. When she did reach him, he began to run again, up toward the house, calling for Willene and Marilyn. He saw as the two women came out of the house.

Willene saw what he was carrying and turned and went back into the house. Harry, Earl and Boggy came from the back of the farmhouse. They'd been cutting wood or in the garden, he wasn't sure. He took the steps two at a time and went into the house with his precious burden.

Willene was setting a blanket down in the living room and had already gotten the medical bag. She'd pulled out a bag of saline and hung it on the standing lamp. Clay gently laid the boy down and he saw Marilyn and Earl setting up lights. Katie pushed through, gasping for air. Her hair was wild and she had twigs scattered on her head.

Willene squirted hand sanitizer in Katie's hands and her own hands. They held up the child's stick like arm and felt for a vein. Willene looked at Katie and shook her head.

"What's the matter?" Clay asked anxiously.

"His veins are nearly collapsed, I can't get a needle in his arm," Willene said.

Marilyn was feeling the child's legs and feet but she shook her head.

"Stop," Katie said dully, and she looked up at everyone with tears shimmering in her eyes.

"He's gone. We found him too late," she said, her voice trembling and she choked back a sob. She turned and Clay caught her and pulled her too him. His eyes were also shimmering with tears as he looked at the faces around him. He bit his lip, trying not to let the pain out.

"Poor little mite, didn't stand a chance," Boggy said softly, his large hand petting the dead boy's head gently.

The room was silent, no one knew what else to say. Earl sniffed and got up, wiping at his face.

"I'll go start a grave for this baby, least ways, he'll have a proper burial."

Clay heard the man softly weeping as he left out of the kitchen door. Clay wiped at his own tears.

"I'll clean him up. I wonder where his parents are?"

"There's no telling. It looks like he's been out there starving, for a while. There is nothing left of him," Harry said softly, his voice thick with emotion.

Clay nodded. Knowing that others were struggling was one thing, but seeing this tiny child, this skeleton of a child tore him to pieces. There was nothing to be done now, except bury the poor thing. This could have been Monroe.

"Poor rabbit, he never had a chance," Willene said softly, wiping her eyes. She began to put the supplies back into the medical bag.

"Where are the kids?" Katie asked, looking around. Clay looked around as well, realizing that Angela and Monroe were missing.

"They are napping thank goodness. I'd hate for them to see this," Marilyn said sadly.

Clay reached over and picked the small body up. It was now heavy in his arms. He felt the weight of it as he carried the dead child to the kitchen. Willene laid a towel on the table and they laid the boy down. She poured warm water into a bowl and she and Clay began to clean the child up.

The boy had blond hair, though it was difficult to see the true color under the dirt and grime. He had pale blue eyes, and a stubby nose. Clay choked back a sob as he held the tiny hand, wiping the dirt from the boney little fingers. Katie came into the kitchen with a small blanket.

"We can wrap him in this when we are done," she said softly. Clay nodded, not trusting himself to speak. They finished up and he carefully wrapped the child in the blanket. Before covering the boy's tiny face, Clay bent down and kissed the child's forehead. Then Willene bent over and kissed him as well.

Clay gently gathered the bundle in his arms and everyone followed him out of the kitchen and out to the graveyard. Earl was there with Boggy, both men digging the small hole for the boy. Clay didn't know why this was killing him. He felt like falling to his knees and never getting up.

He handed the child to Earl, who gently laid the body down in the hole. Clay could see that Earl had been crying, as everyone around him had.

"What should we call him?" Boggy asked.

"Howard." Clay said and broke down crying. He could feel Katie's hand on his arm and he placed his hand over hers and turned into her and held her. His shoulders shook with grief for this child, but also his friend Howard Deets, who'd been brutally murdered.

"Lord, we give you this baby, Howard. Cause we don't know his name. We thank you oh Lord, for let'n Clay find the mite. So's he'd not die alone. That baby is with you oh Lord. We're sorry we couldn't help," Boggy said solemnly.

They each nodded and Earl and Boggy began to fill in the grave. Clay watched as everyone began to leave. He wiped at his face and he looked at Katie. He saw his own grief reflected in her eyes.

"At least he's with us now. He isn't alone," she said softly, and he nodded and hugged her.

CHAPTER NINE

Harry and Clay were in the woods; they'd smelled wood smoke once more. It was well after midnight and they were moving quietly through the woods, Harry had the NVGs and Clay was behind him. It was difficult moving through the dense forest. It had been a horrible day. The loss of the small boy had hit them all hard, but it had really torn Clay apart. The boy had been skin and bones and Harry wondered where the child had come from.

Brian was ahead, but he was quiet, he was tracking and Harry and Clay followed. They were seeing more and more activity. Thanks to the NVGs, they'd seen a large group of people the night before last. There had been twenty people, men, women and children, heading to Beattyville. Everyone had sat on the porch, quiet as Harry softly described what he saw through the NVGs.

They were strung out along the road, walking slowly, someone in the lead had a flashlight, but its beam didn't illuminate very far. Some carried bags, one pulled a wagon behind, filled with belongings. He watched them for thirty minutes until they moved around a curve in the road and out of sight.

"What are we going to do if that happens in the day time? With that many people, and children too?" Willene had asked softly.

"I honestly don't know. I'm hoping firing warning shots will be enough of a deterrent," Harry said softly. He wondered if the small boy had broken away from them and had gotten lost in the woods. There was just no telling.

Clay hissed softly, bringing Harry out of his reveries and back to task. Both men stopped, listening. They heard voices.

"You think they got food?" one man was saying.

"Yeah, I smelled it, and they got women too. I ain't had a woman in fifteen years." The man laughed, but there was no humor in the harsh laugh.

"I ain't believe they let us go," the first man said in wonder.

"Roger, you know them prison guards didn't give a pig's shit about us, they just wanted the food that prison done did have," the man said laughing.

"But Hank, they coulda just let us rot in them cells. They didn't have to free us," Roger said.

"Is you an idjit? They was afraid gubment might come back, and then they'd be charged with murder," Hank said and laughed nastily.

"I don't think them gubment boys is a coming. I think we is on our own," Roger said morosely.

"Yeah, well, that house up there got food and women. We can fuck and eat all we want," Hank said and laughed, choking and spat into the fire.

"Yeah, too bad that lil' boy we snatched got away. We could use him as bait, or even eat him. He was a scrawny thing. Just wished he ain't got away."

"That boy ain't had a lick a meat on him but we could have used him, that's for sure," Hank said and snorted angrily.

"Yeah, they got men up there an they is lots more of them men then me and you," Roger said, worry evident in his voice.

"That is a problem an I've been pondern on it. I was a gonna use that boy, but the little bastard is gone, so all I can come up with is sneak up an get one of them women. Maybe have some fun, and then hold her hostage, and ask for a weapon and then we kill them men. Or better, I seen a kid and a baby. Take them too, we can have fun with them too. Then we pretend we're gonna trade for food and guns," Hank said.

"Makes me wanna get 'em now," Roger said and sniggered low and Hank joined in.

The convicts continued to talk and laugh between themselves. Harry could hear the heavy breathing of Clay beside him. He nudged the man and they moved closer. The brush was thick and they had to move slowly. Harry didn't want to alert the two men.

To Harry, it took forever to get close enough to see the two men. He couldn't see or hear Brian and hoped the dog didn't engage them. At least they weren't armed with weapons. He could now see them sitting before a low fire. Harry noticed the pair wore their prison garb; they were filthy and greasy.

He wondered at the mindset of the guards who'd turned them loose into an already damned world. He shook his head and leaned over to Clay.

"What the hell are we supposed to do?" he whispered.

"I'd say we just kill them where they sit. Those are evil men and there is no telling who they've hurt or killed along the way to get here. We do know they took that child and they mean our children and women harm," Clay whispered back, the rage punctuated every word.

Harry pulled out his Glock, and Clay drew his service weapon.

"I'll take Roger, you take Hank," Harry whispered. Both men stood, lining up their shots, and Harry counted down.

"3...2...1." Both men shot simultaneously.

The convicts Roger and Hank flew back and lay sprawled, away from the fire. Brian whined and went forward; Harry and Clay followed, both aiming their weapons at the downed men. Harry stepped over to Roger, and looked down. The man was still alive, but the life was fading fast from his eyes. The eyes had a shocked look to them, they were wide and frantic and then he was gone. Harry looked over to Hank, and the man was gurgling, blood bubbling out of his mouth and nose, it looked black in the near darkness. The man's feet were in the fire, but he didn't seem to notice it.

"You should have kept on moving along. Now you're dead," Clay said in a voice devoid of emotion. The man sputtered and tried to talk, his eyes wide and then the light of life began to leave and then they went dull.

"Let's leave the bodies here. It is well away from my property. We can come tomorrow with shovels and cover them up, so we don't have to smell them. I don't want to try to do that in the dark," Harry suggested.

"Yeah, thank the Lord and all His wonders, that they lit this fire. We'd not have known; they were too far away from the property for Brian or Charley to detect. At least we know where the child came from. There is no telling where these assholes took him from. I guess it doesn't matter. I'm glad the woodsmoke travels far, and with the breeze blowing just right, we got real lucky tonight," Clay said, shaking his head.

"True enough, I think they could see the house from just above this tree line. They could see the activity without detection. That was too damned close. And why in the hell did the prison release these animals?" Harry said in disgust.

"Make them someone else's problem. You know that bureaucratic bullshit, pass the buck, alive and well in post-apocalyptic America," Clay spat out angrily.

"Yep, I think you're right. Let's put out this fire and head back," Harry said, beginning to kick dirt over the fire. It took a few minutes to make sure the fire was smothered. They didn't need the mountains aflame; they certainly didn't need the farm house burning down. He didn't relish living in the cave, no matter how nostalgic it was.

Two hours later, they returned to the house and Katie was still up; she was sitting in the glider. She got up and Clay came to her and she hugged him. Harry lifted a brow, but said nothing. He'd seen that they had begun to get close. He knew they dated in the past; Willene filled him in.

He was glad Clay had her, and he was glad she was there for him while he was going through all this with the boy and his friend Howard. His thoughts went to the two men. Two animals more like, who'd taken a boy as a ploy to sucker in people. He mentally shook his head.

"I take it from the two shots, you found someone or a couple someones?" Katie asked. The screen door opened and Earl and Willene walked out on the porch. Willene had a tray of coffee cups. Each took one and everyone found a seat.

"We found two convicts; it would seem that the prison system, in all its infinite wisdom has decided to let murderers, rapists, child molesters, and god only knows what, out and free to roam the countryside. They had also taken the little boy, before coming here. They'd brought him and the child had escaped them," Clay said angrily, he took a drink of his coffee and let out a heavy sigh.

"What?" both Katie and Willene said at once.

"So, it would seem, we heard the two convicts laughing about it. It appears they were going to use the boy to get guns and food. Since the child got away, they targeted you women and the kids," Harry hissed low. It still made his blood cold at the thought.

"Oh my god. That poor baby, to spend his last days on earth frightened and starving," Katie said in a voice filled with sorrow.

"The prison let them go instead of being left to die in their cells. They'd been watching this place, from almost a mile away, up on that hill over there, in the woods," Harry said, pointing northeasterly.

"Brian led us to them; we followed the smoke, but Brian was the one who got us close," Clay said, patting the dog, who looked up with a dog smile and his tail thumped the porch's wood floor. Katie leaned over and patted him as well.

"Great, so, now we got to keep an eyeball peeled for prisoners and refugees," Earl said, his speech becoming better, as his mouth adjusted to the dentures and no longer sounded like Sylvester the cat. Harry bit down, they'd had Earl say suffering succotash over and over. He vibrated, trying to tamp down the hilarity, it wasn't appropriate now.

"I can't believe they would endanger the population like that?" Willene said, shaking her head.

"Believe it, I've seen them let less violent criminals out because of budget and overcrowding," Clay said, disgust evident in his voice.

"Those poor people that they come across, they don't stand a chance against those kinds of violent offenders. Nor did that baby. I wonder what happened to his family?" Katie said, worry in her voice.

"They were probably killed, like they had planned for us," Harry said, all internal levity gone now.

Everyone stopped, ahead there were headlights coming their way. Everyone waited, and watched as the vehicle passed and kept going. There was an audible sigh.

"Don't count the good citizens of Kentucky out, many have guns and know how to use them. It has been two months now, and I'm pretty sure they are used to others wanting what they have. These two slipped through, but in the end, we got them," Harry said with satisfaction.

☐

Gene Grady shoved the older man into the president's office. Both Yates and Audrey were smoking cigars, Audrey with his small feet propped up on the desk, his hands resting on his gut. The shirt the president was wearing was a little worse for wear. It was wrinkled and stained. He didn't wear a tie. Yates looked over at him and raised a light red brow in question at Grady.

"I got this here rabble rouser. He was one of the men who shot our guys," Grady said and shoved the older man forward. Audrey shoved back and his feet dropped to the floor, he pulled his chair forward to the desk and leaned heavily on his forearms. He took his cigar out of his mouth, the end chewed badly.

"Is you the jackass that shot my people?" he barked.

The older man didn't answer, but stood tall, at attention. Audrey looked at Yates, then at Grady, his brows lowering.

"Answer the president, old man," Grady barked and gave him a shove.

The older man snorted, looking at Grady and then Audrey with derision, but said nothing.

"Make him talk damnit," Audrey squealed angrily, his face turning red.

Grady turned and punched the old man in the gut and the older man doubled over and let out a gasp.

"Answer the goddamn president," Grady growled again.

The old man straightened slowly, "Sherman, Thornton, United States Marines, serial number..." Thornton began to say and Yates held up his hand.

"Thornton? What on earth are you doing shooting our people?" Yates asked, puzzled.

"Sherman, Thornton, United States Marines." He started to say when Grady hit him in the gut again. Thornton doubled over and vomited onto the floor.

"Stop hitting him in the goddamn gut, I ain't gonna clean that shit up. Sit him down in a chair and hit him in the goddamn face," Audrey screamed, enraged.

Thornton was thrown into a chair, his faded eyes locked on to Audrey, and he grinned.

"What the hell is he a grinnin' at?" Audrey barked.

"A peckerwood," Thornton replied, and grinned, several of his teeth missing.

Yates began to laugh, but it turned into a cough, his bright face turning red. Audrey turned purple and began to sputter. Grady turned and back handed Thornton, causing the older man's mouth to sprout blood from his nose and mouth. Audrey seemed pacified by the action.

Yates stood up and walked to the old Marine; he leaned over at the waist and looked the old man in the eyes.

"Who are you working with Thornton?" Yates asked quietly.

Thornton simply grinned a bloody grin and Yates open hand smacked him hard. Thornton's head rocked back. Grady watched, when Thornton grinned again, he punched the old man in the mouth and three of Thornton's teeth flew across the room, making small clacking noises as they bounced across the floor. Thornton shook his head, as though to clear it. Then he looked up at Grady and grinned, a few less teeth in his mouth.

"Goddamn it, make him talk," Audrey screamed, spittle flying from his mouth, as he pounded his fists on his desk. Yates looked at Grady and then at Audrey and he took the cigar out of his mouth and nodded to Thornton's arm. Grady took the older man's arm and Yate's put the smoldering end of the cigar on the old man's aged freckled arm. Thornton grunted heavily, but said nothing and grinned up at Yates, his eyes glittering.

"Shit," Grady said, he looked at Yates.

"Tell me who you are working with, or it is just going to go downhill from here. You're going to die, you'll either die fast and painless, or you're gonna hurt like all hell," Yates said softly.

Yates watched the old man's eyes and was shocked to see him grin and waggle his gray eyebrows.

☐

Wilber and Boney sat on Boney's porch; both men had tears in their eyes. They'd gotten word that Thornton Sherman's body had been found in the middle of town, a sign pinned to his corpse. It said, *"Turn in whoever is shooting our people and you'll get food and supplies."*

"They done did torture Thornton, but he ain't talked," Boney said, sniffing. "Someone said his last words were Semper Fi. Oorah."

"Oorah," whispered Wilber and blew his nose loudly. Word spread like wildfire that Grady, Yate's lapdog, tortured the old Marine, to make him tell, who'd he been working with to kill Yate's people.

"I was told that those bastards did a number on him. Got burns all over his body, and broke his fingers. They done did beat him to death, but he wouldn't talk. Said he just grinned at them. Dang fool," Boney said and wept even harder.

"That Grady needs a lesson I'm thinkin'," Wilber said, his voice low and deadly.

"I'd say you is on the right track brother." Boney said, his faded eyes filled with rage. They all knew that they could be killed, but someone had turned Thornton in. Someone had squealed and then those bastards killed him, but not before torturing the old Marine.

Boney felt a sense of pride that Thornton had smiled in the face of his own death.

"First, we find that son of a bitch that turned Thornton in, take care of him. Then I think we need to do a little payback with Grady."

"Well Boney, that's the best dang idea you had in a while," Wilber said and lit his pipe. Both men sat back in their rockers, looking out into the distance, each lost in their own thoughts.

Boney knew they faced danger, he'd expected a bullet, but he'd not seen this coming. They'd been so careful, they only spoke among themselves. He knew Wilber's grandson knew, but he was just like his grandpa, a good man. But the bottom line was, someone had turned them in for a meal. That was what their lives were worth nowadays. A meal, a bit of food to stave off one more day of starvation. Would he have done it himself? He didn't think so; he would hunt and trap his own food. He had been doing just that. No, it had to be someone connected with the KKK. Someone who'd seen Thornton go out at night with his long gun.

They'd have to check and if they couldn't find him, then Grady would provide the answers they needed, quid pro quo.

Vern groaned, he'd fainted, but he was coming around now. He could smell something cooking and he gagged; he knew it was him. Heavy saliva hung like wavering ropes from his mouth. He heaved and heaved, nothing but acid came up. He heard Hobo sniggering and then he heard Bella May hush him. Tears fell down his hot cheeks, but he kept his eyes closed. He didn't want to see his missing forearm. He trembled; she was indeed Karma.

All his life he'd been an angry man, and he'd been an angry child. He'd not even known what he'd been so angry about. Here and now, he'd gladly live the rest of his life smiling and being kind to others. If only he could get the hell out of the basement with his limbs intact. That wasn't to be. He took a deep breath and cracked one eye open, he saw the stump of his left elbow and shut his eye. More tears cascaded down his face and he felt them hit his naked thighs.

"Are you hungry Hobo?" He heard Bella May ask.

"Sure am, fill me up Karma," he said.

Vern shook his head, he wondered if he'd go insane like Hobo, maybe that wouldn't be so bad. Hobo seemed a hell of a lot happier now than when Vern had arrested him on other occasions, in another world, in another time and in another life. Hobo had been a bully, Vern knew, he was one himself. He enjoyed the power, he enjoyed their fear, it was like a drug. Now here he was, being eaten by a crazy serial killer; she'd been here doing this for years. How did they not know about her?

He felt a cool hand on his shoulder and jerked up, looking into Bella May's eyes. They were frightening, they held no remorse, no empathy or sympathy. The smile on her face was mechanical; the only time he'd seen her truly smile was just before she began to harvest meat. Then there was an inner glow about her.

"I've made you a bowl, though there isn't any meat in it. You need to eat, to keep up your strength," she said kindly, though Vern knew it wasn't kindness, it was a well-rehearsed play.

He began to heave again, the muscles in his stomach jerking and contracting, but nothing came out but the nasty saliva. He watched her walk away through tears. *Karma indeed*, he thought.

CHAPTER TEN

Vern sat quietly in the dark, he could hear Hobo's breathing. He knew the man was awake. Their days were spent in the dark and the chill of the basement biting into their naked flesh. There were times he couldn't tell if his eyes were open or closed. It had become a game, are they open, are they closed? He snorted to himself.

"Vern? Is you awake?"

"Yeah Hobo, I'm awake."

"You ever think we'll get out of here?" Hobo said in a wistful voice.

"Hobo, you ain't got no more feet, she done ate 'em."

"Oh yeah, I forgot. How's your foot?"

"It's gone Hobo, remember?"

"I know that, it just when she done did hit you with that hammer, sounded bad."

Vern sighed heavily, they had this conversation nearly every day, yet he had no idea how many days had passed. The only time they saw light, was when Bella May came to feed them or eat them. He shivered in remembrance. She'd come down yesterday he thought, and was going to take his foot. She'd already taken both of Hobo's.

He'd wiggled his foot, trying to keep it out of her grasp. She'd huffed and got up. He thought with his heart leaping with hope, that she'd leave him alone. She'd come back with a large hammer and had brought it down with incredible force, onto the top of his foot.

He shivered violently at the memory. He'd screamed and screamed, spit and tears flying from his face. He'd voided and even now felt the stinging heat to his face. He'd not fought her and had blissfully fainted when she began to cut the bone.

"You there?"

"Yes Hobo, where else would I be?"

He wondered at Hobo's mental stability and almost envied the man's lunacy. His leg throbbed at the site where his foot use to be.

"Are ya gonna fight next time?"

"No, I won't. I think that damn hammer hurt worse than the saw."

"Yeah, sounded like it."

They were quiet for a while. Their breathing filling the chilled room. He felt like crying. He always felt that way now. But it was no use. There was no one but Hobo to hear his tears nor care for that matter.

"You know Vern? I's sorry you is here, but I'm glad I ain't alone."

"I know Hobo, I'm glad I'm not alone."

"Is you scared of dying?"

"Not of dying, no, of workin' my way there though. Piece by piece."

"Yeah, I know what'cha mean," Hobo said and sniggered.

More silence and Vern was about to nod off when Hobo cleared his throat. Vern waited, he knew what was coming.

"Vern?"

"Yeah Hobo?"

"Can you tell me a story?"

"No."

"Pleasssssseeeeee."

"Okay, fine. Once upon a time…"

"Ohhh I like them once upon a time stories," Hobo said and giggled.

"Once upon a time, there was these two hunters, and they was huntin up in the hills, just up yonder."

"What was they hunting?" Hobo asked excitedly.

"Bear."

"Ohhhh, I like bear, like ta eat it too."

"Anyway, them two good old boys, they were good hunters," Vern continued and heard the soft weeping of Hobo in the cool darkness, and he felt his own tears slide warmly down his own face.

☐

David and Gideon sat in the darkness of the mine. It was even quieter without the children. But David would take that silence over the weeping of mothers for their hungry children. Everyone sat eating, their meals had become better down in the coal mine, but it wasn't from the guards, who continued to send down as little food as they could get away with.

The people coming back to the coal mine in the evening, smuggled fruits and vegetables back into the mine, to supplement the remaining people's food. They'd been told they could bring food back, but most of their food had been confiscated by the guards. So, everyone still brought food back, they just hid the majority of it.

David and Gideon did without; they'd agreed to give over what they could smuggle in. They planned to give the food to the others left behind. At the Friedhof's farm, the workers were eating well. Unfortunately, they didn't go every day, so whatever they could smuggle back had to last the others.

David and Gideon made do with the rations that were sent down. Julia was grateful for the extra food, and she'd been happy that her children were safe and eating better. But she was still broken up about being separated from them. David couldn't blame her, it was a great sacrifice on her part, to let her children out of her sight.

David was worried; some of the people down in the coal mine had developed coughs. He could hear Stroh. That wasn't good. They once more requested more masks, the others wearing out. He'd gotten some bandanas from Jutta; he could at least pass them onto those who needed them. They had to get their hands on some weapons; the guards above were heavily armed.

Gerhard only had a hunting rifle, but he said he would see what he could do. David was on the fence; Gerhard and his family were already taking a big chance on hiding Mary and the children. If he brought attention to his farm, David was afraid for Gerhard's family and the children as well as Mary. There had to be some way to smuggle weapons into the mine.

"I've been trying to figure out a way for us to get weapons down here. I really don't like Gerhard getting them. That could bring trouble to his family and the children," David said.

"If the mayor hadn't confiscated most everything, I don't think it would be a problem; as it stands now, it is hard to get hands on anything more than a pitchfork," Gideon said, taking a bite of a withered apple.

"Maybe if we can get word out, secret of course, that if we could get small arms, we could arm ourselves and perhaps when we go up for the ride to the farm, we could ambush the guards," David speculated.

"Some of those boys have automatics. They'd cut us down in a skinny minute. Perhaps if we did some kind of multi-layered attack?" Gideon said.

"That could work good, but again, we need to find weapons, and without getting anyone caught or killed," David said shaking his head. He'd bathed at the farm, but even after a few hours in this cave, he could feel the oily grit seeping into him. If he ever got out of here for good, he'd start using firewood and not coal. They'd all thought about escaping once they'd gotten to the farm, but that would endanger the others left behind.

The mayor was clamping down; some of his men had been killed, picked off. David smiled at that. The more of them they could take down, the better odds they had, but it also had a negative effect. It pushed the alert up and all eyes watching. Everyone was afraid, and fear permeated the citizens. People were starting to turn on each other for food, selling their neighbors out for bread. Word had filtered down to the mine about a marine who'd been beaten to death, for information about who'd been picking off Audrey's people, and the kid that was shot for giving the mayor the finger.

People were afraid and it reminded David of way back when, when people were accused of being communist, or back farther, during the Salem witch trials. It was a witch hunt then and it was a witch hunt now, and if you didn't like your neighbor, or wanted his home or his food, why tell the mayor that your neighbor was one of the shooters, or harbored blacks. People lost their integrity; they became greedy and the mayor was pitting people against each other. He was offering food as a reward for turning in a friend, a neighbor.

At some level David could understand, and if he had children, or for Mary and her baby, what would he be willing to do? How far would he go to protect her and her unborn baby. He was almost ashamed, because he would do damn near anything. It was a fine line to walk and to judge.

☐

Alan drove the truck along the back roads. He had a few boxes of food in the back. He was now looking for the family he and his grandfather had come across some time before. He pulled over when he came to the neat little shack. He once more saw the woman and her three children there. He was glad to see them, they looked good. His grandfather had been right, they'd lived with very little and so hadn't felt much of the bite of the EMP.

The woman stood, looking at him. She had a hoe in her hand and her children gathered behind her. He got out of the truck and took off his hat and smiled. He saw her shoulders relax and she smiled back at him. She turned and whispered something to the children and they turned and ran.

"How you doin ma'am?" he asked and nodded.

"Fair to middlin," she said and smiled.

"Ma'am, I come cross some wayward vittles." He smiled impishly at that and snickered. He could feel his face turning red and the woman laughed outright.

"Did you now?"

"Yes'um. I took the liberty of packin a few and brought y'all family some. I figured the mayor won't miss none what he don't know."

The woman laughed now, true humor creasing her face. It melted the years of hardship and she was quite pretty. Alan's smile broadened.

He turned from her and let down the tailgate of his truck. He pulled a large box out; it was filled with flour, sugar, coffee, rice, pasta and dried beans.

"May I come up?" he asked politely and at her nod, he walked around to the side of the yard and walked up a broken set of steps. They were old and in disrepair, but held his weight.

He followed her to her home and she opened the door. Alan stepped in and it was gloomy

233

without lights but he could see well enough. It had a small living room and even smaller kitchen.

"You want me to put it in the kitchen, Ma'am?"

"Sure, sit it on the counter, son."

He did so and as he was turning, a large man filled the doorway. Alan squinted to see the man's features, but they were hidden in the shadows. The man came forward and seemed to fill the very room. He held a shotgun in one hand, though it was pointed at the floor.

"Young'uns said we had a visitor," he said, his voice deep and gravelly. Alan could feel it rumble in his chest.

"This here's the boy I told you about, with his grandpa. They'd warned about the mayor's goons," she said.

The man held out a large hand and Alan took it, his bony one disappearing into its grasp. Alan thought the man could easily rip his arm off and tried not to snigger nervously.

"Yes sir, I done brought some things, figured the mayor wouldn't miss 'em." Alan did snigger then, and once more his face heated up.

"We're much obliged son, thank ya kindly," the big man rumbled. Once more, Alan could feel the rumble through his chest. It made him feel calm for some reason. He liked that.

"Well sir, ma'am, I'd best be gettin on, got more deliveries."

They all walked out of the small house, and Alan made his way to the steps. The woman came forward and gathered Alan in her arms for a hug. He could feel his ears burning and knew they were turning bright pink. He grinned foolishly and turned and went down the steps, nearly tripping over his feet.

He pulled the tarp back over the other boxes and got back into his truck. He lifted a hand in farewell. Turning the truck, he drove away, a smile still planted on his face. They seemed a nice family and he was glad they had their daddy there. He sure was a big man and Alan knew that the family would be safe. He doubted anyone would want to tangle with that giant. His own hand had felt tiny in the man's grasp.

He kept driving until he came to some homes. Most of the places had broken windows and open doors. They looked hopelessly abandoned and he wondered what had happened to the families that lived there. It saddened him to think they'd died or perhaps they were in the coal mine. He saw a house, coming up and saw all kinds of lawn ornaments.

He smiled, they were those gnome things and he laughed. He pulled into the driveway. The grass was long and uncut, but he knew no one would waste gas for mowing. He got out of the truck and pulled down the tailgate. He retrieved a box, and walked up the sidewalk to the house.

He juggled the box as he knocked heavily on the door. He could hear movement inside and waited patiently. The door cracked open and he saw a green eye looking at him. He smiled pleasantly and the door opened more.

"Good afternoon, ma'am, how are you?"

"Oh, I'm doin fair. What can I do for you son?" she asked smiling at him.

"Ma'am, I have some vittles for you. I come across some extra food, and figured I'd share a bit," he said and grinned.

"Well, isn't that just sweet of you. Come on in," she said opening her door wider.

Alan walked in and looked around. He saw a buffet that had been knocked over, and he frowned.

"Ma'am, did you have some trouble?" he asked with concern.

"Oh, that's been a bit of time. Some nasty man had come by to take what wasn't his."

"Is you okay?" Alan asked in concern.

"Oh, I'm fine now. Thank you, son," she chirped happily, her green eyes bright and merry.

"Can I at least set it ta rights?" he asked her.

"That would be so kind of you son, yes, thank you," she cooed.

"Yes'um, and I like your chicken apron," he said laughing and bent to lift the heavy furniture upright. It was heavy and he shifted his weight. Then he felt something hit him on the back of the head.

☐

Boney had taken it upon himself to hunt down the bastard who'd turned in Thornton. He dressed carefully in rags, dirtying up his face. He planned to wander over to Thornton's home and pretend to be digging around the neighborhood, looking for food. He'd act like someone with no sense, feeble and weak.

He carried a long and lethal knife; he planned to get some answers out of the little bastard. It was early evening; he'd not wanted to be too noticed and by the time he got to Thornton's home, it was near dark. He shambled along at a slow pace, and he scanned the area, and he looked surreptitiously around. He saw several people sitting in lawn chairs outside their homes. They looked thin and there was a fire, and they sat staring in it. They didn't look at him as he passed.

He kept walking, and saw other lights in homes, candles. He saw shadows and silhouettes moving around inside. As he drew closer, he heard laughter coming from a house; it was two down from Thornton's home. Laughter was a rare sound nowadays and so he figured he'd move a little closer to investigate.

He went toward the back of a house, and moved along the back yard. He was three houses down from his target house. He slowed down, his ears on high alert. He didn't need to get his ass blown away from some homeowner. He didn't hear any dogs and moved faster. He came to the house and he could clearly hear two men. They were laughing. It was full on dark now and Boney stood back away and stood on a cinder block to look into the window.

There were three candles lit, and two men sat at a table, it looked to be a dining room table. He could make out other chairs around it. He scanned the room and other windows, but he didn't see anyone else moving around. One man was holding something up and laughing. When Boney saw what it was, the blood began to heat in his veins. It was the Marine Corps flag and the man was laughing, making a scarf out of it.

Boney's hands tightened into fists and the bones popped and snapped. His lips pulled back into a silent snarl. He saw other items on the table, he saw several boxes of food. The men were drinking beer. He smiled savagely. He'd let them have their fun. Let them drink. They already sounded half drunk. Then later, he'd sneak in and show them what happened to people who betrayed a Marine.

He let the cool air around him ease the heat that was radiating through his body. The smile stayed in place as he thought about what he was going to do to those two men. His hand caressed the knife he now held in his hand. His thumb flicked over the sharpened blade and he grinned as he felt the trickle of blood from his thumb.

Gerard, Richard, Bill, David and Gideon sat at the farm table drinking coffee. They had finished the day's work and Jutta was working on dinner. The men were about to leave to go back to the coal mine, but David had asked them to have a talk.

"Richard, Bill, you are the only two who can help us as I see it," David said, looking at the men. They looked back at him nervously.

"There is no way that we can get those people out of the mine without your help. There is no way we can get weapons. It is just too hard, and I really don't want Gerard and his family helping because that puts a lot of people in danger."

Richard and Bill looked at each other and David could see the fear in their eyes. He knew that they were afraid, but they were all afraid.

"I think we can maybe get our hands on a couple. But that president got tight control now.

Yates is watching everyone. He's sore mad about all them killins goin on."

"There are normally only four guards when we leave the mine and when we come back. Not always the same ones. How well do you know them?" David asked.

"I know a couple of 'em, Reece Archer and Tommy Schip. They's real scumbags. They been taken a lot of the food for themselves. Any one try to bitch about it, they get hurt or they family get hurt," Richard said darkly.

"So, if you or I have to kill them, it won't break your heart?" David asked, smiling.

Bill and Richard laughed at the same time; it wasn't a pleasant laugh. Apparently, they'd been crossed by the men. Again, David wondered how many people were disgruntled with the status quo. This could work in their favor.

"Do you think that perhaps you could talk to some of the men who are tired of the bullshit? Maybe sway them to our side?" David asked.

Everyone jerked around when they heard a cry from upstairs. Jutta came around the table and ran into the hall. Everyone stood and looked as Mary came down the stairs. Her face was pale, and her mouth moving but no sound coming out. David looked at her and then saw the blood on her dress. He almost fell, walking toward her. She was bleeding, she was losing the baby.

☐

Wilber sat across from Boney; both men were smoking their pipes. Wilber noticed that Boney had several bruises around his face and his knuckles were bruised. Both men sat quietly and Wilber waited for Boney to talk. In Boney's hand was a flag, it was the United States Marine Corps flag. He knew that it was Thornton's. Both men rocked quietly, and Wilber heard the distant hammering of a woodpecker. It echoed around the holler.

Wilber could smell smoke in the air, and then he heard a distant shot. It sounded like someone was hunting up in the mountains. There would be more and more of that. He'd gotten a rabbit this morning and later when he got home, he'd fried it up for him and Alan. He'd not seen Alan in a day or two. He knew the boy was out delivering food to people. He smiled when Alan told him about Andy Anderson's truck and the food in the back.

He was proud of Alan; the boy was growing into a fine young man. His mother would be proud of him as much as he was proud of the boy. He smiled softly. He shook his head, that kid had been through more in the last couple of months than he had in his first few years in the military.

"Got some good intel," Boney said, bringing Wilber back. He looked up at the man and smiled.

"Good, if ya think you is up to it, tell me what happened Boney, I wanna know."

Boney let out a long sigh and Wilber smiled and watched the man settle back for a long tale. He put a wrinkled and knotty hand up to hide a smile. He too sat back and got more comfortable.

"I was a standing out in their yard. I was watchin' those two peckerwoods guzzlin' beer. Them bastards was disrespecting Thornton's flag and things. So, I waited, real patient," he said and laughed, deep and angry.

"Bastards," Wilber said angrily.

"Yep. Them pecker-heads was drunk as a skunk; guess they got paid in beer. A good man's life for a fuckin beer. When they passed out, I just walked myself in. I tied them bastards up and set to cuttin on them," he said and sniggered.

A deep smile creased Wilber's face, he felt great satisfaction. He knew Boney was good with a knife. He could make a stone talk.

"First bastard sang like a bird. I only made one cut across his gut and he was happy to sing. Said that the other shithead was the one that turned Thornton in. Said that shitbag said he was sitting out and saw Thornton come in early mornin, figured something was up."

Wilber sat forward, and he could feel his vertebrae pop; it was becoming interesting and enlightening. He wondered if it was the last job they did. He needed to keep that in mind when he came home from the next hunt.

"The booger-eater that squealed on Thornton finally came to, and so I got some names from that little bastard. Reece Archer, Jeff Bluemont, Tommy Schip, Darrel Mopes, Bobby White, Morty Greer, Murphy Tweet, and Ralph Finch. He said them boys is tops in the KKK along with Audrey, Yates, Smalls, and Grady."

Wilber whistled, that was some damn good intel. They needed names.

"That's damned impressive. Are there anymore names?" Wilber asked.

"Boy said he thought they was others, but he ain't know who they was. Course I ain't believe him, so I just jiggled the knife a lil," Boney said, his eyes dark with suppressed rage.

"I take it he had more to say?" Wilber asked.

"Yeah, said they got some safe house with the bulk of food and weapons. But, said he didn't know, said he weren't high enough on the food chain. I poked a bit more, but the boy done cried and cried he ain't know. I believe him, by then, I'd cut most of his fingers off," he said laughing hard and Wilber laughed as well. He shook his head, he was proud of Boney, he got the intel they needed.

"Good man, how'd ya leave it?"

"Cut both their necks and set the house afire. Got a bunch of supplies and weapons out of there afore I torched it. I went over to Thornton's and got his things. Got his medals, his uniform, the flag," he said holding up the flag. His voice was now filled with emotion and Wilber could feel his eyes sting from the tears that were coming. Their comrade in arms had been dealt a shitty death, but he'd stood up to the bastards and hadn't broken.

There were very few men out there with that kind of grit anymore. Most were cowards, willing to sell their pride for an easy life. They'd take from others without a second thought, thinking it was owed to them. Even before their world went dark, people wanted the money, but they didn't want to work for it. They felt intitled to what you had, felt if you had money, you should share it with them. He grunted. No, his friends were a rare breed and one just died, keeping them safe.

"We'll hold a special ceremony for him. It'll be secret, just us boys. Just his true friends. Then, we'll go get us some damn payback," he said in a low guttural voice.

Made in the USA
Monee, IL
16 November 2023

46774289R00136